To Skipper and Hugh

Love Mary

Christmas 1965

LISTEN, THE RED-EYED VIREO

LISTEN, THE RED-EYED VIREO

BY MILTON WHITE

Introductory Poem by Ogden Nash
Illustrations by F. B. Modell

DOUBLEDAY & COMPANY, INC. GARDEN CITY, NEW YORK

To Allene Talmey,
with gratitude

All of the characters (except the birds) in this book are fictitious, and any resemblance to actual persons, living or dead, is purely coincidental.

Portions of this book have appeared in *Vogue*

Library of Congress Catalog Card Number 61-9567

Printed in the United States of America

CONTENTS

UP FROM THE EGG: THE CONFESSIONS OF A NUTHATCH AVOIDER

By Ogden Nash

Bird watchers top my honors list.
I aimed to be one, but I missed.
Since I'm both myopic and astigmatic,
My aim turned out to be erratic,
And I, bespectacled and binocular,
Exposed myself to comment jocular.
We don't need too much birdlore, do we,
To tell a flamingo from a towhee;
Yet I cannot, and never will,
Unless the silly birds stand still.
And there's no enlightenment in a tour
Of ornithological literature.
Is yon strange creature a common chickadee,
Or a migrant *alouette* from Picardy?
You rush to consult your Nature guide
And inspect the gallery inside,
But a bird in the open never looks
Like its picture in the birdie books—
Or if it once did, it has changed its plumage,
And plunges you back into ignorant gloomage.
That is why I sit here growing old by inches,
Watching the clock instead of finches,
But I sometimes visualize in my gin
The Audubon that I audubin.

I

The First of Spring

At a quarter to seven I saw my first bird of the morning. There on the trunk of a large ash tree: a sparrow? a nuthatch? What was it Miss Folger-Robinson had told me moved *upward* around the trunk of a tree?

With trembling fingers I ruffled through the pages of Peterson's bird guide; then I saw the bird fly from the tree trunk and vanish behind the corner of Scott Hall. With relief, I slipped Peterson into the pocket of my army field jacket, and, clutching my umbrella, I continued on my way to the Hurlburts' house and my first walk with the Olney Bird Watchers.

I was a "new young man" in English at the University, and Miss Folger-Robinson, white-haired and gentle, was determined to open doors for me. As senior member of the Olney Bird Watchers, she had sponsored my membership in the group, although I really knew nothing about birds.

The campus, as I crossed Slant Walk, was on the edge of waking. The overcast morning tinged the red brick buildings with gray, through which a few lighted dormitory windows glistened. A damp wind swept through the bare branches of the trees outlined against the sky. I huddled into my field jacket and recalled that I had forgotten to wear my gloves. I thought of going back for them; but the bells in the tower built by Beta Theta Pi struck seven, beginning the official campus day. I was late.

A brown creeper! I thought suddenly. *That* was what Miss

Folger-Robinson had said moved *upward* around the trunk of a tree.

I hurried across Oak Street and down Arbor Lane, where the unexpected smell of wood smoke filled the damp air.

Moving vigorously in slacks and wool shirts, the retired Physical Education teachers, Miss Wills and Miss Barrett—one of them tall and gaunt, the other short and heavy-set; I never could tell who was who—tended the burning of an enormous pile of brush in their yard, on the opposite side of the ravine. I waved to the Physical Education ladies, but they did not see me.

As I rang the Hurlburts' doorbell I realized that I had neglected to take my binoculars from the case during my walk to Arbor Lane—a bird watcher is always prepared—and I fumbled anxiously to get them around my neck before the door opened. My umbrella fell to the ground. My binoculars slipped from my hand. I made a wild grab for them and caught them by the strap.

The door opened. Miss Folger-Robinson called out, "Good morning! Welcome!" The smile on her weathered face wavered for a second as she took in the umbrella and the dangling binoculars. Then, collecting herself, she said warmly, "Come in. We've been waiting for you."

I followed her into the living room. Several logs burned in the Hurlburts' fireplace. On the long, low table before the fireplace stood a coffee percolator and a platter of powdered doughnuts. Two wide picture windows, one facing north and one facing east, opened the room to a winding ravine.

In front of the picture windows squatted the Olney Bird Watchers, binoculars around their necks. Everyone in the room turned to look at Miss Folger-Robinson and me—like birds perched on a farm fence, I thought; I blushed at my irreverence. I saw the club members stare at the umbrella which I held nervously.

Mrs. Hurlburt, dressed in blue, came toward me, smiling. "Put your things here," she said. She slipped the umbrella out of my hand and quickly buried it under the pile of clothing on the bench beside the fireplace. "And have some coffee and doughnuts."

"As soon as you've finished your coffee," Miss Folger-Robinson said to me, "we'll go for our walk."

Dr. Hurlburt, president of the Olney Bird Watchers, shook

my hand. "I hope we have more luck outside than we've had in here. You know all the club members, don't you?"

I nodded. I glanced around the room: Mr. and Mrs. Ingraham (Miss Folger-Robinson had briefed me that Ingraham's Ph.D. thesis had investigated parasites in coots); Strether—an associate professor in Zoology; Hunt—a young graduate assistant, working on bird *songs*. I hesitated for a few seconds when I came to the two tiny, gray-haired ladies, affectionately known in town as the Gnomes. One of them taught Latin. They were heavily tweeded and wore knitted tams.

Miss Folger-Robinson must have noticed the pause. She whispered to me, "The *Talcott* sisters."

I cleared my throat, made an attempt to say cheerfully, "Hello, everybody," and felt I succeeded only in producing a vague

cracked sound. Fumbling, I poured myself a cup of coffee and shook powdered sugar from the doughnuts onto the carpet.

With sinking heart and with precariously balanced coffee cup I surveyed the Olney Bird Watchers, who had turned their backs to me as they peered once again through the picture windows into the ravine. Never before, it seemed to me, had I seen people so obviously Trying to Make the Best of Something. Was it my presence as a new member?

My binoculars weighed heavily around my neck. I sipped hot coffee and told myself I did not belong. Outside, a light March rain began to fall. On the opposite side of the ravine Miss Wills and Miss Barrett were still busy at work, tending their burning brush pile. I saw them look up at the sky anxiously, as if trying to estimate whether they could beat the heavy rain that threatened. A gust of wind swept into the brush pile and sent a thick cloud of smoke flying into the gray air. A mourning dove that had perched on the Hurlburts' feeder fluttered away with a whirring sound.

I said cheerfully, "Miss Wills and Miss Barrett are doing a good job of cleaning up their side of the ravine."

The nine other members of the Olney Bird Watchers turned as one and stared at me. Miss Folger-Robinson, closest to me, hurriedly reached out for the coffeepot on the table before the fireplace. She said to me, "Have some more coffee . . ." When she saw that my cup was still full, she stood beside me helplessly.

Mrs. Ingraham, her hands folded over her obvious pregnancy, simply said, "Humph!" Mr. Ingraham pretended to clean the lenses of his binoculars; the small piece of tissue tore in his fingers.

I saw Miss Wills, across the ravine, motion energetically to her co-worker. Miss Barrett stalked toward a branch lying on the ground, lifted the branch into the air, and tossed it onto the burning brush pile. Both women paused in their work to look up once more at the light rain that fell.

Mrs. Hurlburt sighed; she picked at an invisible piece of lint on her blue dress.

Strether said, "Perhaps they could do a less thorough job, eh?" He forced a laugh. The other bird watchers nodded. The Gnomes looked at each other sadly for a second. Hunt turned away from the window abruptly. He held his empty coffee cup out to Miss

Folger-Robinson and said, "Perhaps someone should have spoken to them about the brush pile last month, when they bought the house across the ravine."

Miss Folger-Robinson filled his cup, grateful, I thought, for something to do. Mrs. Hurlburt picked up a thick, leather-bound notebook from the desk, turned the pages, found the entry she wanted, studied it quietly for a moment, and said, "Here's the list of birds we saw at our first meeting last year." She drew her index finger down the page. It was obviously a long list.

"What do we have on our list so far today?" Strether asked. "Not much, eh?"

Mrs. Ingraham said, "Starlings, mourning doves, sparrows, and a blue jay."

The Gnomes shook their heads at each other and shrugged. Dr. Hurlburt ran his hand over his thin gray hair. He said to me, "Some really wonderful birds used to come to our feeders."

Mrs. Hurlburt moved toward the window. The ravine was obscured by smoke from the brush pile. "If only Miss Wills and Miss Barrett weren't so *active, all* the time," she said. "I thought they were *retired* ladies."

"Now, my dear," Dr. Hurlburt said.

Miss Folger-Robinson drew me aside. She said quietly, "Towhees and song sparrows built nests in that brush pile every year. And just last Wednesday, Miss Wills and Miss Barrett chopped down an old tree stump in which a screech owl lived. Have you ever seen a screech owl?" Miss Folger-Robinson cupped her hand as if she were holding a bird in it.

Mrs. Hurlburt called out bravely, "There are plenty of doughnuts. No one seems to be eating."

"I think we've all finished," Miss Folger-Robinson said to her. Her voice became brighter. "Perhaps we could start our walk now. We'll do better on the trail, away from all the smoke."

The Olney Bird Watchers rose to their feet, adjusted binocular straps, clutched Petersons, and brushed powdered sugar from their clothing.

"Time for the baby," Mrs. Ingraham said to her husband.

"Do you want me to help you, dear?" Ingraham asked, following her.

Startled, I watched the pregnant Mrs. Ingraham shuffle down the front hall toward one of the bedrooms. I attached the Ingrahams' nonchalance to the fact that Mr. Ingraham's field was zoology: birth was a casual affair.

"Well!" I said, heartily.

"Is everyone ready?" Dr. Hurlburt asked.

I looked out at the thin drizzle soaking the dismal morning; for just a second I glanced longingly at my umbrella lying on the bench beside the fireplace. Strether, Hunt, Miss Folger-Robinson, and the Gnomes, shoulders thrown back, heads erect in spite of the rain, were already standing in the front yard, waiting.

"We're ready," Mrs. Ingraham said, stepping out of the bedroom. On her back, papoose-fashion, she carried a smiling round-faced baby, perhaps a year old. She saw me staring, and she smiled.

"My daughter Kathy," she said. "You can't start a bird watcher too early. Off we go, fore and aft!" She patted her stomach and shuffled past me. The baby fastened to her back grinned, head bobbing.

My shoulders thrown back resolutely, although no one could have noticed since my army field jacket was a couple of sizes too large for me, I followed the Ingrahams outside into the drizzle, without my umbrella. On the north side of the house Dr. Hurlburt took the lead down a steep path into the ravine. On the slope opposite us, peering through the smoke, the Physical Education ladies waved an ax and a rake in the air and, as they worked, called to us cheerily, their voices echoing through the ravine, "Operation cleanup! Neither wind nor rain . . ."

Dr. Hurlburt waved back and tried to smile. Mrs. Ingraham said, "Humph!"

Indian file, we started out along the trail at the bottom of the ravine, heading toward Wander Creek. The leafless trees looming on the slope were a dead gray-brown color against the heavy drizzle. The binoculars hanging around my neck thumped against my chest. Rain blurred the lenses of my horn-rimmed glasses. I found myself alone at the end of the line of bird watchers.

The only sound in the gloomy morning was the scuffing of feet through wet leaves. I took off my glasses, tried to wipe them dry, then, trudging along after the others, I cupped my hands over my binoculars to ward off the gray rain.

The baby, Kathy, joggling along on Mrs. Ingraham's back, smiled up at me from under the dripping brim of her little hat.

Miss Folger-Robinson, in the front of the line, stepped aside to let the other club members pass her; she fell into line again beside me. The shoulders of her jacket were wet, but she seemed not to notice.

She whispered to me, "It was right here that the screech owl used to live." She held her hands in the air, palms turned upward, to indicate emptiness.

Ahead of us Dr. Hurlburt had stopped. His voice as bleak as the rain falling in the ravine, he said, "Do you remember what we used to find here each year?"

I found myself staring with sadness at the hacked roots of a tree stump. Mrs. Hurlburt placed a hand on her husband's arm. The Gnomes whispered to each other and looked about the ravine, turning their heads slowly, in unison, as if they were following the silent flight of an owl.

Strether said to me, "A quiet morning, eh? Not very impressive for you." To the others he called, "Let's see if we can rustle up something interesting for our new member!"

Hunt said, head tilted, "I don't even *hear* anything."

For a moment everyone remained silent, listening for a stray bird song. I heard only the splatter of rain against the trees. A drop of water trickled down my neck.

Dr. Hurlburt glanced upward at the leaden sky. "It may rain," he said. He shrugged and started walking along the path that led through a grove of pine trees and maples. Everyone trailed after him, dodging wet branches. I was last in line. Chilled, I fastened the collar button of my field jacket.

"I hope the rain holds off," I said, dabbing at my face with my already soaked handkerchief. My glasses had blurred again, hopelessly.

In front of me Miss Folger-Robinson nodded and strode after the group, her head turned slightly, ready to catch any sound of a bird. The wetness of the leaves and trees became part of the silence that hung over us. Even Wander Creek, running slowly through its limestone and clay banks, seemed wetter than usual.

Wendell Hunt raised his hand. Instantly the Olney Bird Watchers halted, listening. Hunt shook his head. "I thought I heard—" He shook his head again.

I saw the Gnomes glance at each other and smile. One sister

reached into her jacket pocket and held up an Audubon bird caller. "Shall I try calling them with this?" she asked Hunt. Her voice had in it a touch of mourning dove with laryngitis.

Hunt nodded solemnly. The Audubon bird caller squeaked and twittered as Miss Talcott twisted it. Huddled in a group, heads tilted, alert, the Olney Bird Watchers waited for a response to the call. The rain beat against the trees, against the wet leaves on the path, and against the surface of Wander Creek. All else was silence.

Miss Talcott tried again. The Audubon bird caller twittered. We listened. Silence.

After a few moments of waiting Dr. Hurlburt said, "Well, I guess it *is* raining, after all."

I nodded. Then, as pointedly as possible, I said to the Ingrahams, "I hope the baby doesn't catch cold."

Mrs. Ingraham swung around so that Kathy faced me. The baby gurgled contentedly under the dripping brim of her hat. Mrs. Ingraham said, "She loves it."

Mr. Ingraham chucked the baby under the chin. "But we have no birds to show her," he said.

I brushed away the raindrops hanging on the brim of the baby's hat.

Mrs. Hurlburt said, "The coffee at home is still hot, and we have plenty of doughnuts."

Dr. Hurlburt turned up the collar of his jacket. He looked defeated. "We'll follow Wander Creek to Route 27 and walk back along the road," he said.

In silence, heads lowered, shoulders rounded to ward off the rain, the Olney Bird Watchers sloshed after him through tall wet grass. The bird walk was over: none of us any longer listened for sounds or watched the trees. My shoes and the cuffs of my trousers were soaked.

As we crossed the open meadow and approached the highway I saw a passing car slow down while the occupants stared at us. Two boys in the back seat, their faces pressed against the rain-splattered window, gaped at us until the car disappeared over the hill.

Mr. Ingraham took his wife's arm. Hunt, for a second, raised his head, listening, but the sound he heard was only the distant humming of the tires of a pickup truck speeding toward us on the wet road. I braced myself against the spray that swept off the truck as it passed us.

"Hot coffee will taste good, eh?" Strether said to me.

The Gnomes, walking behind us, whispered that the rain would at least help discourage the awful brush-pile fire that Miss Wills and Miss Barrett had started.

"We've always seen so *many* birds on our first walk," Mrs. Hurlburt said. "Do you realize that this time we haven't seen *one?*"

At the top of the hill, where Oak Street came into Route 27, Dr. Hurlburt led the way across the old Hilsinger place, taking a short cut toward Arbor Lane. Rain fell steadily. As I plodded on I took off my horn-rimmed glasses and held them close to my chest while I tried to wipe them dry. The binoculars hanging around my neck were flecked with rain; I wanted to ask Miss Folger-Robinson, who strode in front of me, if rain would injure the binoculars. I called to her, "Will the rain—"

I almost collided with her. Suddenly the line had been halted by Dr. Hurlburt, who raised his hand in warning. I hastily finished drying my glasses, put them on, and peered in the direction in which Dr. Hurlburt pointed. "There!" he whispered. "There!"

A robin, its beak filled with dried grass, sat in the old apple tree on the edge of the Hilsinger front lawn. Instantly all binoculars were focused on the solitary bird.

"A robin," Mrs. Ingraham said. She turned sideways so that Kathy, behind her, could see. Mr. Ingraham gently turned his daughter's head until he was sure she was looking at the robin.

I said, "It's *my* first robin this spring," and I remembered the day each spring of my boyhood when I saw the first robin of the season; and I could remember the sense of renewal I always felt in my heart.

The robin darted out of the apple tree and perched on the sagging cornice over the old Hilsinger doorway.

"Nest building in March," Dr. Hurlburt whispered excitedly. "The warm spell last week probably speeded him up."

The robin burst into song. The Gnomes, standing on the edge of the road, murmured to each other without once lowering their binoculars. The other members of the Olney Bird Watchers, binoculars focused on the robin, smiled dreamily to themselves.

I wondered what Kathy would recall someday of a moment in the chill March rain when, for the first time in her life, she had watched a robin build its nest.

I raised my binoculars again and focused them on the robin. A Plymouth coupé speeding along Oak Street swerved to avoid hitting the Gnomes in the road. The startled driver blew his horn, fiercely.

"Well, now!" Mrs. Hurlburt said. Her face, with rain beating against it as she watched the robin, was aglow with pleasure.

Suddenly one of the Gnomes, on tiptoe, approached the apple tree, took a piece of string from her pocket, and, reaching upward, draped the string over a branch and backed away.

The robin swooped down from his nest and perched on the branch. For a few seconds he stared at the Olney Bird Watchers;

then with his beak he picked up the piece of string, and flew back to his nest.

"Splendid!" Miss Folger-Robinson whispered.

As if at a signal each of the Olney Bird Watchers took from his pocket a piece of string and in a group started on tiptoe toward the apple tree. One of the Gnomes came back to me and handed me a piece of string. I found myself tiptoeing forward with the others. We hung the pieces of string on branches of the tree and stepped back, watching.

The robin, without hesitating, swooped once more into the apple tree. My heart beating, I watched the robin pick up *my* piece of string and fly back to his nest. Mrs. Ingraham turned to me and smiled.

Again and again the robin returned to the tree, until finally he had collected all the string.

"Splendid, splendid," Miss Folger-Robinson whispered.

As the Olney Bird Watchers started walking toward Arbor Lane, Mrs. Hurlburt placed her hand tenderly on her husband's arm. I looked up at the dull, wet sky. The acrid smell of wet smoke rose from the smoldering brush pile across the ravine. The Physical Education teachers were no longer in sight.

An idea began to take shape in my mind. I hurried forward, fell into step with the Hurlburts, and said to them, "Why don't we build a brush pile on *your* side of the ravine? I mean, pile up brush for a new home for the towhees and song sparrows. We might even bring an old hollow tree stump into the ravine for the screech owl."

The Hurlburts and the other bird watchers stared at me. I stumbled along beside them, my heart sinking.

"Isn't it possible?" I asked, peering at the group through my rain-splashed glasses, trying to understand their silence.

Mrs. Hurlburt said, "For heaven's sake . . . !"

"But of course!" Miss Folger-Robinson cried.

Strether said to Hunt, "I think I know where there's a tree stump—"

Rain beat down on us.

Mrs. Hurlburt said to her husband, "We can build a wonderful new pile of brush."

"We'll all help," Mrs. Ingraham said enthusiastically, shifting Kathy to a more comfortable position.

Miss Folger-Robinson looked up at the sky. Rain dribbled from her hat and trickled down the back of her jacket. "Why not begin right now!" she said.

"To the ravine!" Dr. Hurlburt cried, leading the way.

The Olney Bird Watchers surrounded me, and together we strode after the Hurlburts. Suddenly Hunt raised his hand. "Listen!" he said. His face brightened in the rain, and he gestured backward, toward the apple tree on the old Hilsinger place. The robin had begun to sing again, over and over.

Smiling, the Olney Bird Watchers stopped to listen.

II

The Great Blues

"Secrecy," Ingraham said, "is of the utmost," and he glanced ominously at the Olney Bird Watchers.

His words wove the group into the deliciously solemn mood that accompanies being let in on a secret without having to reveal any secrets of one's own. Standing there at dawn with the Olney Bird Watchers at the edge of Johnston's Woods, ready to begin our weekly bird walk, I remembered the movie *Beau Geste*—Beau and his friend had become secret brothers by exchanging blood from cuts they made in their wrists. Could I suggest that we . . . ?

"Follow me," Ingraham said.

The fantasy burst. In a group, trailing Ingraham, the Olney Bird Watchers plunged into Johnston's Woods.

"I haven't a clue as to what it's all about," Miss Folger-Robinson whispered to me. In front of her, to indicate that they, too, knew nothing, the Gnomes shook their heads negatively, or rather they seemed to rub their heads together like a pair of mourning doves. Ralph Strether and Wendell Hunt, vexed with Ingraham's secrecy, listened for birdcalls.

Dr. Hurlburt said to his wife, "Remember, dear, the barred owl we saw here two years ago?"

Ingraham said quietly, "I'm not going to show you a barred owl."

No one, I decided, could be more superior than a bird watcher leading other bird watchers to a discovery.

Binoculars ready in her hands, Mrs. Ingraham turned to us and said, rather proudly, "Even *I* don't know." To her husband she said, "It isn't just some old coots on the lake, is it? He *loves* coots," she added.

"But we already have coots on our list this spring," Mrs. Hurlburt said.

"It isn't coots," Ingraham said, serenely.

"In the movie *Beau Geste*—" I said. But I did not continue.

Miss Folger-Robinson pointed to the baby in the carrying-bag fastened to Mrs. Ingraham's back. "Kathy's asleep."

Strether giggled. "She's bird sleep-walking, eh?" he said.

The Gnomes smiled generously. I glanced at the sky. In the east the sky held the promise of a bright day; but in the west a vast grayness pressed down against the bare trees of Johnston's Woods. "It's going to rain," I said.

Then, as I spoke, the sun rose above the eastern horizon, filling the sky with the new bright red of dawn; I saw that the vast grayness in the west was really only the tail end of night. A bird walk at dawn was still new to me: I had a lot to learn about the sky.

I watched the rays of the rising sun touch upon the remainder of night in the west. The drabness began to fade until suddenly it was gone completely. The entire sky turned pale blue, clear and clean. Nor, in this new light, were the trees as bare as I had thought at first. The tall beeches and maples showed the trace of green buds, an assurance of spring bursting out once again. The greenery seemed almost to be breathing the fresh morning air. Everywhere, everywhere, Johnston's Woods was carpeted with the blossoms and the new green leaves of spring beauties and Dutchman's-breeches.

Mrs. Ingraham kneeled, respectful of her pregnancy extended in front and her baby daughter Kathy tied to her back; she spread her hands over the pink and white blossoms of the spring beauties. "Every spring," she said.

The two Gnomes—I corrected myself, the *Talcott* sisters—pointed to a dog-toothed violet they found at the foot of a maple tree.

"I'm no good with flowers," Strether said. "I can't even tell the difference between Dutchman's-breeches and false corn, or is it called squirrel corn?"

"You mean crowfoot?" Mrs. Hurlburt asked.

Miss Folger-Robinson stooped and touched a blossom. "Does the difference matter?" she asked.

Miffed by the interruption, Ingraham ostentatiously took his bearings. "We go on that way," he announced, pointing in the direction of the lake that glistened in the sunlight beyond the edge of the woods.

Hunt said irritably, "Botanists on a bird walk!"

"Humph!" Mrs. Ingraham said, rising.

We fell into a group again and trailed after Ingraham and Hunt. Overhead the sky had become a deep, new, morning blue, cloudless. I breathed the fresh air and watched the greening branches of the tall trees outlined against the clear light of dawn.

Ingraham came to a halt before the huge fallen trunk of a beech tree. The exposed roots seemed still to be fighting for life, waiting for a strong hand to turn the trunk upright again into the wide sandy cavity where the tree had once grown.

"We're almost there," Ingraham said, his tension increasing. He turned his head from side to side and listened in a wide arc, not for birds, I decided, but for the surety that the Olney Bird Watchers were alone. In as dramatic a whisper as he could achieve standing in the woods on a clear and glorious spring morning, he said, "Once again, secrecy is of the utmost. Remember, not a word to anyone else." He shrugged. "Otherwise—"

Otherwise—I saw us all toppled over, roots exposed, like the old beech tree.

In silence we followed Ingraham. The Gnomes held their binoculars clutched tightly in their hands. Hunt and the Hurlburts and Strether pretended to be nonchalant.

Miss Folger-Robinson whispered to me, "What can it be? Can you . . . ?" And when Ingraham signaled for absolute silence Miss Folger-Robinson left her question unfinished and frowned at me, as if *I* had been the one talking.

At that moment Ingraham began to gesture wildly toward the stand of huge beeches ahead of us. I scanned the lower branches of the trees, searching for movement. I grasped my binoculars ready to train them on the first sign of a flutter. In the distance, beyond the beeches, sunlight sparkled bright and clear on Johnston's Lake.

Ingraham whispered tensely, "Uuup! Look *up!*"

I realized he meant us to look up, into the tree*tops*. Unnerved, I asked, "What? What? Where?"

Then I saw a bird rise and flap, float, glide—I could not decide which—from the top of one of the beeches. "Good heavens!" I exclaimed. "Storks!"

"Good heavens!" Dr. Hurlburt cried. "Great blue herons!"

A second bird left its nest far at the top of a beech and, huge wings slowly flapping, raised itself into the air and glided over the lake.

Miss Folger-Robinson said breathlessly, "Of course. Great blues!"

"Seven in all," Ingraham said, his voice quivering. "I discovered them yesterday. A heron rookery!"

"They do look like storks, don't they?" Mrs. Ingraham said.

I glanced at her, and my heart warmed with friendship. The Olney Bird Watchers had trained their binoculars on the two herons that soared lazily over the beeches. The Gnomes danced with delight. The herons, returning to the treetops, settled onto their nests. Three other herons rose, flapping hugely, to glide toward the lake and then back over the beeches.

Dr. Hurlburt lowered his binoculars and tried to control his excitement. "Some people," he said, "call them cranes, which is a mistake, of course. The crane flies with its neck extended *out*. You can see that the heron flies with his long neck tucked *back* into his shoulders. That's the difference."

"They're so prehistoric-looking," I said. I glanced down at myself. I was still dressed in field jacket and corduroy trousers: I had almost expected to find myself wearing an old bearskin or leopard skin.

"They're the largest birds I've ever seen," Miss Folger-Robinson said. "They *do* look prehistoric, like pterodactyls or something, I can never remember."

"Seven of them, you said?" Dr. Hurlburt asked Ingraham.

"Seven," Ingraham said.

"Listen for their call," Hunt said, ecstatically. He scanned a page of Peterson and reported that the heron's cry was supposed to sound something like *frahnk, frahnk, frawnk.* "I hope we get a chance—"

"They're in the egg-sitting stage, obviously," Dr. Hurlburt said. "They mustn't be frightened from their nests, not at this time."

"They're our first great blues!" Mrs. Hurlburt said. Her voice implied that unless we pledged ourselves to secrecy they might be our *last* great blues.

"They'll need absolute privacy," Dr. Hurlburt said.

"Absolute," Ingraham said, taking the stance of a sentinel. The Gnomes anxiously surveyed the woods for intruders, then, satisfied, focused their binoculars once again on the herons as the birds sailed over us crying suddenly, *frahnk, frahnk, frawnk. . . .*

The sound echoed over the empty woods. Hunt's eyes gleamed; his hand shot in the air, as if he would reach up and touch the sound.

Mrs. Hurlburt stepped backward, slightly pale. "We're disturbing them," she cried.

I looked up quickly at the herons' nests, half expecting to see eggs and birds come tumbling down, the rookery ruined.

Dr. Hurlburt raised a steady hand. "Quiet, everybody! Freeze for a minute."

The Olney Bird Watchers froze for a minute. The herons circled in the air, glided back to the beeches, and finally, wings extended, settled on their nests. Without speaking Ingraham waved his hand in the air signaling us to turn and start back toward the station wagon. On tiptoe we turned, wordless, our heads lowered, as if by not looking at the herons we could add to the silence of our departure.

Sunlight, bright now, picked up the myriad blossoms of spring beauties and Dutchman's-breeches. Rising above the carpet of spring flowers, waxy May apples glistened in the morning light. Everywhere the shrubbery burst with new green foliage. I glanced backward. A single great blue heron rose majestically from a nest and sailed into the air, its long neck folded back into its shoulders, its legs trailing behind. I looked away guiltily.

Ingraham halted beside the uprooted beech tree. The Olney Bird Watchers drew a deep breath.

"Well!" Miss Folger-Robinson said.

We clustered around Ingraham, who said with strained casualness, "I found them by accident as I was sitting at the edge of the lake watching coots. I thought at first—" Instead of telling us what he had thought at first, he waved his arm in a broad motion that portrayed the enormity of the surprise he had experienced.

"Positively prehistoric," Miss Folger-Robinson said.

A black and white chickadee perched on a branch of an oak tree and observed us nervously.

"A chickadee in the oak tree," I said, pointing.

No one paid any attention to me or the chickadee.

"How big *are* they?" Mrs. Ingraham asked.

Hunt ruffled through Peterson. "It says here they're about four feet tall."

Still wearing his air of triumph, Ingraham turned to his wife. "Did Kathy see them?"

"She slept through them," Mrs. Ingraham said.

"Good grief, Lydia!" Ingraham said.

I lowered my head and looked up into Kathy's face. She was asleep, smiling; and I thought a child's face had all the time in the world for everything.

Mrs. Ingraham said to her husband, "She'll have another chance to see them, dear."

"Dear," Ingraham said, "every trip back here is a potential threat to their sense of security."

Dr. Hurlburt nodded vigorously. "Secrecy," he said, "is of the utmost."

"Absolutely," Strether said.

Suddenly, from the distant grove of trees that marked the edge of the road, came the cry, "Ping, ping!" A dozen Cub Scouts of Troop 16, knapsacks on their backs, trampled into view, led by Mr. Dale, their scoutmaster.

Ingraham swallowed. Mrs. Hurlburt murmured, "Good heavens . . ."

Mr. Dale caught sight of us gathered beside the uprooted beech tree; he hurried toward us, while the twelve Cub Scouts, all of them shrieking, followed their leader in a gallop over Dutchman's-breeches and spring beauties.

As Mr. Dale approached he shouted to us, "Seen anything interesting? Anything good?"

I said hello to the one Cub Scout I recognized, Kenny Watson, whose father was in the English Department. "How are you?" I asked.

"I'm by no means fine," Kenny said. "I'm hungry!"

Mr. Dale held up a finger. "We don't eat for another hour," he said. Beaming, he asked Ingraham again, "Seen anything interesting?" He gave Kenny Watson a slight push. Kenny had been staring much too obviously at the pregnant Mrs. Ingraham. "We camped out in the picnic area last night, our annual sleep-out."

"We're hungry!"

"In an hour, men," Mr. Dale said, waggling his finger.

The dozen Cub Scouts leaped into the uprooted beech tree and with prolonged wails swung from the branches, pretending to be Tarzans.

From the vicinity of the lake in the distance I heard a faint *frahnk, frahnk, frawnk*. Mrs. Hurlburt, hearing the herons' cry, turned pale. Miss Folger-Robinson, her hand trembling, tucked a strand of gray hair under her broad-brimmed hat and said, "Oh dear." The Gnomes steadied themselves against a tree.

Mr. Dale poked a finger at Ingraham and persisted, "Seen anything interesting, anything we can pick up for our nature walk?"

I watched Ingraham struggle with his conscience. He glanced at the dozen shrieking Cub Scouts who clambered over the beech tree, ripping branches.

I said hurriedly, "We haven't seen anything." Then, pointing to the spring flowers around us, I added, "By the way, can you or any of the boys tell us the difference between Dutchman's-breeches and false corn?"

"Some people call it squirrel corn or crowfoot," Miss Folger-Robinson said quickly.

"Boys, boys!" Mr. Dale shouted. "Don't tear branches off any of the *living* trees!"

A titmouse fluttered past us and perched in a nearby maple.

Young Kenny Watson raised the stick he held, aimed it rifle-fashion at the titmouse, pulled an imaginary trigger, and yelled triumphantly, "Ping, ping!"

In horror the Olney Bird Watchers stared at him.

"Ping!" Kenny Watson yelled again.

The titmouse flew off.

Ingraham caught his breath, but he said coolly to Mr. Dale, "Have the boys seen the coots on the lake? I think they'll enjoy them. Come along, I'll show you where they are."

"Boys!" Mr. Dale shouted. "Boys!"

Ingraham started back to the road, leading the group in the opposite direction from the heron rookery. "Coots," he said to the cluster of Cub Scouts who trailed after him, "are what you might mistake for black ducks with white bills. They're fine diving birds. Watch for that. And when they take off from the water . . ."

Still shaken, the Olney Bird Watchers followed at a distance. At one point the Gnomes paused to whisper excitedly to Miss Folger-Robinson, who, I thought, tried to calm them.

I said to Strether, "Perhaps the boys could have been trusted with the secret of the herons. Scouts are supposed to be loyal and friendly and all those things."

"Last year during their sleep-out," Strether said, "the kids were given beer by one of the fraternities picnicking around here. The kids told everyone in town about *that*."

Miss Folger-Robinson called us to a quiet halt in a patch of sunlight. She whispered, "Miss Talcott and her sister have a wonderful idea." She waited for a moment, until Ingraham and the Cub Scouts had walked on a short distance out of hearing: then she continued, "They've suggested that from now on, when we refer to *them*"—she pointed in the direction of the great blue herons—"we'll call them simply G.B.H.'s. No one will know what we're talking about. Unity in secrecy," she added.

"Ping, ping!" Kenny Watson shouted in the group ahead.

"Heaven help us all," Mrs. Ingraham said.

"Heaven help the herons," Mrs. Hurlburt said, pale again.

Three days later, on Tuesday afternoon, Miss Billings of Botany, tall, flat-heeled, and friendly, cornered me during faculty tea, and boomed, "I hear you bird watchers had a problem out at Johnston's Woods last Saturday. Well, well!"

Had she heard about the herons? I corrected myself: about the G.B.H.'s? A chocolate-chip cookie crumbled in my fingers.

Miss Billings boomed on, "Not knowing the difference between Dutchman's-breeches and false corn! Little Kenny Watson told me about it."

"Oh," I said, relieved.

"Don't feel bad," Miss Billings said. "What're you doing after the tea? I'm going out to Johnston's Woods. Come along, I'll show you the difference between the two plants—that's the best way to learn.

"You bird watchers are too specialized," she added.

Half an hour later I was hurtling down Browne Road toward Johnston's Woods in Miss Billings' station wagon. In a cloud of dust Miss Billings pulled into the parking area adjoining the picnic grounds; she sprang from the car and called out to the woods at large, "Now, then!"

I trotted after her as she led the way toward the nature trail. She halted at the foot of an oak tree and swung her arm in an encompassing gesture that included all the fresh green carpet of spring flowers that covered the ground.

"Genus, *Dicentra*," Miss Billings announced. "All of it is *Dicentra*. That's why you've been confusing the squirrel corn with the Dutchman's-breeches. They have the same genus, the same leaves. It's the *blossom* that provides the distinguishing field characteristic."

She kneeled, and her fingers probed the blossoms. "See here?" she said, beckoning to me.

I kneeled beside her and peered at the blossoms.

"The lobe of the blossom of Dutchman's-breeches is round. Here, can you see? Now the lobe of the blossom of squirrel corn is *pointed*. See the difference? Dutchman's-breeches, rounded; squirrel corn, pointed. It's simple.

"Now, then. Kenny Watson says you got crowfoot mixed up with these flowers. You were way off. Come along here." Miss Billings scanned the woods and plunged toward a maple a few feet away, where she kneeled again. "Here, now. You use the name crowfoot for this, but that's really a misnomer. It's really toothwort or pepperroot. But"—she fixed her eye on me accusingly—"it should never be mistaken for either squirrel corn or Dutchman's-breeches. It isn't the same family at all. The *real* crowfoot belongs to the buttercup family, while toothwort is related to the mustards."

Miss Billings rose. "All straightened out?" she asked brightly. "It's always best to *see* the plants in their habitat."

"They're clear now," I said. "I'll—" I stopped.

I heard the sound at first only faintly in the distance; then the cry grew louder: *frahnk, frahnk, frawnk!* Miss Billings turned her head and looked upward.

"Genus *Dicentra*, isn't that what you said?" I asked her hastily.

"What?" Miss Billings said.

"*Dicentra*," I said.

Miss Billings nodded absently.

"It's a beautiful afternoon," I said. I pointed to the trees outlined delicately green against the blue sky. The spring sunlight threw short clear shadows over the woods. The afternoon smelled of new green leaves.

Frahnk, frahnk, frawnk! The sound was louder than ever. Miss Billings stooped down and flicked a twig from her shoe.

She pointed to a dogtooth violet growing in the shade and said casually, "This isn't a violet at all, of course. It's really a lily. Fawn lily or trout lily is its real name, because of the spots on the leaves."

"How interesting," I said.

Miss Billings straightened, fixed me with steady eyes for a couple of seconds, then said, "I think you can keep a secret. You can, can't you?" Without waiting for an answer she beckoned me to follow her; then, after holding a finger to her lips for silence, she started through the woods.

Toward the G.B.H.'s, I thought, my heart beating fast.

For the first time I noticed the sign of a trail stamped through the spring plants that covered the ground. Beside the uprooted beech tree, Miss Billings halted. "Secrecy," she whispered to me, "is most important. I'm counting on you to tell no one about what you're going to see. Now, then."

A moment later Miss Billings pointed triumphantly to the grove of beeches outlined against the sparkling water of Johnston's Lake. Miss Billings whispered, "Look up there."

A pair of herons rose heavily from their nests, legs trailing behind them. The birds flapped luxuriously through the air. "Great blue herons," Miss Billings whispered to me. "I came across them a few days ago, but I haven't breathed a word about them, in order to protect them. Magnificent, magnificent." Miss Billings' voice trembled with admiration for the herons sailing overhead.

"Magnificent," I said.

Miss Billings glanced at me, and her face glowed with the deliciousness that comes of sharing a secret.

That evening, in Rini's Grocery, I saw the same glow appear in Miss Folger-Robinson's face as she entered the store and caught sight of me. In passing she placed her hand on my arm, winked, and whispered, "The G.B.H's."

Should I tell her about Miss Billings? Miss Folger-Robinson's smile brimmed over. I decided to remain silent.

As enthusiastically as I could I replied in a whisper, "The G.B.H.'s."

A secret is a secret, I thought, collecting my groceries.

"*Fagus grandifolia*," Mr. Branford said, on Friday afternoon, as he and I tramped through Johnston's Woods lugging firewood to the picnic area for the faculty spring cookout.

"I beg your pardon," I said. I had been listening intently to the distant *frahnk, frahnk, frawnk* of the G.B.H.'s. I wondered if the darned herons *ever* kept quiet. I felt a slight wave of indignation.

Branford patted the trunk of a beech tree. "*Fagus grandifolia*," he repeated. "Beech."

Branford taught dendrology.

"Well," I said, "would you repeat that once more?"

Branford had not been listening to me. Instead he continued speaking, "Beech is a climax tree in this area. Maple is another of the climax trees. Good solid trees, but they mark the end of a cycle." He nodded in the direction of a low tree that bore large new green leaves. "There's one of my favorites," he said, "*Asimina triloba*. Papaw."

Our arms full of firewood, we plodded back to the picnic area. None of the faculty had arrived as yet for the cookout. "We're doing well," Branford said, starting back into the woods. "All we need now is kindling."

I noticed that as Branford spoke he seemed distracted, nervous. He asked me, "Do you get out to Johnston's Woods very often? It's a nice place for quiet walks."

I told him that the Olney Bird Watchers went there about twice a month.

"Yes?" he said. "Well." He wrinkled his forehead. He pointed absent-mindedly to a redbud tree. The pink blossoms caught and reflected the sunlight. "You know the redbud?" he asked. "*Cercis canadensis.* And the tulip tree over there? *Liriodendron tulipifera.*"

Branford stomped unseeing into a huge network of cobwebs that hung between two trees. Preoccupied, he brushed cobwebs from his face and asked, "On those bird walks of yours do you find much of interest, usually?"

I stalled. "In March we saw a red-breasted nuthatch—"

Branford continued brushing cobwebs off his face. "A red-breasted—. Well, I wouldn't know anything about *that.*"

All at once he turned to me, fixed me with a steady eye, and said, "You look as if you can keep a secret. You can, can't you?" He paused. "Come along then."

My heart sank. *Good heavens,* I thought, as I trotted after him.

Branford hurried ahead of me through shadows and sunlight that played over the Dutchman's-breeches and squirrel corn covering the ground. I wondered if he would pause beside the uprooted beech tree to caution me about the need for secrecy. He did. He raised a warning finger and said, "Don't forget, what you're about to see has to be kept a deep secret." Then he advanced through the woods with long strides, his hand raised for silence. Suddenly he pointed and whispered fervently, "There! Up there!"

I saw several blue herons floating through the air over the beech trees. Wings extended, necks drawn back, legs trailing behind, the herons appeared to me, for the first time, to be handsomely indifferent to what was happening on the ground below them. They never looked down at us, at all. They appeared simply to be busy *being* great blue herons.

I glanced at Branford, who radiated excitement as he said, "I found them here a couple of days ago. They're great blue herons."

"G.B.H.'s" I said.

"Huh?" Branford said.

Overhead, the great blue herons glided through the air minding their own business; they arched their enormous wings, hovered for a long moment above the beech trees, and one by one settled down onto their nests.

Wind touched the high tops of the beeches and maples surrounding us. Sunlight flickered over us. Branford breathed again, his face beaming.

A fellow needs a secret, I thought.

In silence Branford and I turned away from the heron rookery and started back to the picnic area. Faculty members had begun to arrive; half a dozen cars were parked beside the road. A softball sailed in a wide arc between Rogers and Benecke in Geology. I remembered, as Branford and I emerged from the woods, that we had intended to gather kindling for the cookout fires.

"The kindling," I said.

Branford hurried away, calling to me, "Perhaps we can do without it. I'll try starting the fires with the wood we have."

Kenny Watson slid to a dusty halt before me, his Cub Scout cap askew on his head. He raised a finger, aimed it gun-fashion at the darting shadow of a bird, and cried, "Ping, ping!" Suddenly he said, "You been to see the herons?"

I gaped at him. Then, crushed, I aimed a finger at him. "Ping, ping," I said.

Kenny's mouth opened. I walked away, with dignity, to meet Miss Linn, who had just pulled into a parking space on the road.

Miss Linn was a new member of the English Department; she had light brown hair and blue-green eyes. I waved to Miss Linn, and she waved back. As we strolled away from the parking area for a walk through the woods before the picnic, I heard a heron's cry, *frahnk, frahnk, frawnk!*

I paused; and the next moment, helpless, I heard myself with a mixture of guilt and delight, saying to Miss Linn, "You look as if you can keep a secret. You can, can't you? Remember, secrecy is of the utmost. Come along."

Her blue-green eyes glowing deliciously, Miss Linn followed me.

III

The May Count

At four-thirty on the morning of the May count rain began to fall. It beat against my window, waking me, and as I lowered the pane wind swept cold raindrops onto my hands.

I decided gratefully: they'll postpone the bird count.

Miss Folger-Robinson would be heartbroken. At this moment she was probably at home staring crestfallen out at the rain, Peterson's bird guide and binoculars in her hands, the May count ruined by bad weather.

On the previous Thursday, when she reminded me that the Olney Bird Watchers were to devote their walk to the May bird count, she had explained, "This'll be the peak weekend for warblers."

"My first bird count," I said.

"You'll enter into the spirit, once you begin," Miss Folger-Robinson said. She put down the shears with which she had been clipping grass around her tulip bed. "One of these days I'll get you *really* interested in birding," she said to me, with the shadow of a smile. She moved her hand gently in the air, as if she were turning a knob. "It's like opening a door. You'll know when it happens for you."

A few minutes before five, even before the alarm sounded, I leaped out of bed, peered out at the gray morning, and saw that the rain was only a steady drizzle. I decided to get ready.

When I stepped outside the street was silent in the drizzle.

The morning was cold for May. I hoped my old army field jacket and cap would keep me dry. I slung my binoculars over my shoulder.

Up the street Miss Folger-Robinson's house was dark; her garage door was open and her car gone. Blossoms beaten off her redbud tree by the rain lay scattered over the sidewalk, and I crossed onto the tree lawn to avoid stepping on them.

I hurried along the three remaining blocks to Upham Hall, at the edge of the campus. The Olney Bird Watchers huddled under the trees in front of the science building. Miss Folger-Robinson, her shoulders hunched against the rain, wore a brown leather jacket, which more than ever gave her the appearance of a robin. Her familiar, battered, wide-brimmed hat protected her head from the rain.

She strode toward me, excitedly. "It's on!" she said. "We've just decided not to postpone." She looked up at the gray sky. "A bad morning, but it may clear, it may clear." She guided me to the center of the group.

"It's his first bird count," she said to the others. "He's nervous."

Strether and Hunt nodded at me. The Gnomes clucked sympathetically, trying to put me at ease.

"Well," I said, and I moved closer to Strether and Hunt, to see what they were doing.

They had spread between them a map of the countryside, over which they pored like generals planning a campaign. I saw that the map had been marked off into sections and numbered. Strether pointed a finger. Hunt leaned closer over the map. I heard them mumble plans, alter decisions, check with Dr. Hurlburt, and finally agree. Strether, in charge of the May count, turned to survey the group huddled in the drizzle. Miss Folger-Robinson, I thought, stood at attention. The wide brim of her hat flapped in a gust of wind that swept through the trees.

His spectacles and his round face blurred with anticipation and rain, Strether announced final plans: we would begin birding at McGonigal Pond, then go on to the airport for the bobolinks and the owls, then to the area around the formal gardens, and finally to Johnston's Woods.

Watch the roadside for birds, he warned; remember, not only species, but the *number* of each species—he paused, and I thought he eyed me, waiting for the importance of what he said to catch

up with me—which meant, he elaborated, still watching me, that it was necessary to record not just *some* redwings, but the actual *count* of redwings.

Miss Folger-Robinson glanced at me, and her glance implied she had faith in me. Touching my elbow, she guided me toward the station wagon.

The Ingrahams came running toward us—Mrs. Ingraham, alarmingly pregnant now, lumbering along with Kathy fastened to her back in the canvas carrying-bag.

"I decided at the last minute to come along," Mrs. Ingraham explained, breathlessly. "This will probably be my last bird walk for a while."

Ingraham noticed my concern. "The doctor says we have another week, at least," he assured me.

Strether looked up at the sky, as if accepting the challenge of the rain; with a wave of his hand he directed us once again toward his station wagon. "Mrs. Ingraham," he said, "can be our recorder." He handed her a card and pencil.

As she took over her duties Mrs. Ingraham pushed back her shoulders proudly. The Gnomes adjusted Kathy's hat so that the rain did not hit her face. Kathy smiled at the Olney Bird Watchers.

"Sweet," Mrs. Hurlburt said, her voice tender.

I said to Mrs. Ingraham, with a touch of anxiety, "Better keep bundled up dry."

Mr. Ingraham pushed at his horn-rimmed glasses. "She never listens to anyone about weather," he said.

At that moment Miss Folger-Robinson, pointing wildly in the direction of a clump of bridal wreath bordering the sidewalk, cried, "Stop! A hummingbird! Ruby-throated!"

I was too late to see it.

"My first of the year," Miss Folger-Robinson cried triumphantly. "Did you notice the color of its throat? Like flame."

"Mark it down," Strether said to Mrs. Ingraham.

"One hummingbird, ruby-throated," Mrs. Ingraham said.

Almost before the doors of the station wagon were closed Strether released the brake and we careened down the road toward McGonigal Pond, four miles away.

Miss Folger-Robinson said to me apologetically, "It'll be helpful if you keep your window open. Will the rain bother you?"

She brightened, "A hummingbird, at the very outset! We'll be lucky this morning, in spite of the weather."

Rain dripped through the open window and soaked my jacket sleeve.

Miss Folger-Robinson continued hurriedly, "I raised a hummingbird last spring. Mrs. Hogan brought me a nest she found on the ground, under her hydrangea. One of the baby birds in it was still alive." Miss Folger-Robinson cupped her hand, as if she held a baby hummingbird in it. "Getting that little thing to eat! Nothing seemed to work, until finally I mixed honey and water, put some on a geranium blossom, and held it out to the bird. *Down* went its tiny bill into the blossom. Wonderful, wonderful.

"He ate that way for weeks, honey on a geranium blossom. I wanted to band him before I freed him, but you can't band a hummingbird, I found. Practically no tibia."

Strether sped along. "One flicker," he said, without slowing down.

Mrs. Ingraham made a notation on the check list.

Hunt tilted his head. "I hear a Tennessee warbler off there on the left," he announced.

"Our first warbler on the May count," Mrs. Hurlburt said.

Desperately, I began to scan the countryside. The rain beat in on my face. We passed a plowed cornfield. A flock of birds rose from the furrows. I shouted, "Grackles! Over there! I know grackles."

Strether said, rather grimly, "*Bronzed* grackles. How many were there?"

One of the Gnomes nudged me. I looked down at her hands. She held out eight fingers.

"Eight," I said, feeling gratitude for the Gnomes sweep over me along with the rain.

Strether jammed on the brakes—we all fell forward—while at the same time he rolled down his window, raised his binoculars, and ignored the protesting horn of the heavy truck that screeched to a halt behind us. The Olney Bird Watchers leaned out the side of the station wagon, binoculars focused on a telegraph pole just ahead of us.

"Got it!" Strether said with satisfaction. "One sparrow hawk." He rolled up his window and sped off, unmindful of the still-protesting horn from the truck.

"You didn't see the hawk," Miss Folger-Robinson said to me, sympathetically. "Well, another time."

At McGonigal's Pond, Strether swung off the main road and came to a halt in a field that bordered a swamp. The Olney Bird Watchers piled out of the station wagon into the rain.

A cold wind blew over the pond. Ingraham paused to dry his glasses. The Gnomes fastened the buckles on their galoshes. Mrs. Hurlburt tied a kerchief over her white hair. Strether and Hunt had already forged ahead, and we trailed along after them like a brood (I found myself thinking in bird-world terms). At the edge of the pond Strether raised his binoculars and surveyed the gray choppy water.

"Ready?" Strether said to Mrs. Ingraham.

She raised her pencil to her recording card.

"Two blue-winged teal, two lesser scaup, and eight . . . nine . . . ten coot," he reported.

Dr. Hurlburt and Hunt nodded in agreement as Strether called out the species.

"*Eleven* coot," Hunt corrected.

"Eleven," Ingraham said.

I caught in my binoculars the vague gray outlines of what looked like simple ducks to me. Leaning toward Miss Folger-Robinson, I whispered, "Which are which?"

She opened her Peterson's bird guide to the wind and rain and tried to show me pictures of the birds which Strether had called off and which Mrs. Ingraham recorded.

"I'm not so good at water birds myself," Miss Folger-Robinson said; "that's why it's such fun birding with Strether. He knows them."

"But he goes so fast," Mrs. Hurlburt murmured.

Mrs. Ingraham said to her husband, "You record for a while, dear. I'd like to see the blue-winged teal."

Before she could raise her binoculars, however, Strether had started tramping away from us, through the brush surrounding the swamp.

Mrs. Hurlburt said to me, "That's what I mean."

We sloshed after him, over soggy hummocks and through mud.

"It would have been nice to *see* the blue-winged teal, wouldn't it?" Mrs. Ingraham whispered to the Gnomes, who, looking half-frightened at Strether, seemed relieved that he had not heard.

In the east the sky had lightened, but directly over us a dark cloud released a sudden last shower. My trousers were soaked up to my knees (most of the time, now, I associated birding with rain-soaked clothes). Swamp mud clung to my shoes. Strether and Hunt stalked on, leading the way over a series of half-rotted planks thrown down over the hummocks. Miss Folger-Robinson strode after them, followed by the Gnomes and Ingrahams and Hurlburts. By the time my turn came to cross the planks the boards were covered with slippery mud. I hesitated.

Miss Folger-Robinson called back to me, "We have to move quickly if we want to get species!"

Moving sideways over the boards, I kept myself hunched almost double.

A dark flash of feathers rose with swift wingbeat from the cat-tails near me. Startled, I teetered, slipped onto all fours, and

looked up only in time to see the flash of feathers vanish in the brush.

Strether cried, "A least bittern! First I've seen here at McGonigal! Did you notice the buffy wing patches?" He waved his arms enthusiastically in the rain. "Good birding, group! Mark it down, Ingraham!"

I pushed back my cap from my eyes. My binoculars seemed to weigh a ton around my neck. With water oozing through my shoes I squashed cautiously along after the other birders.

Ingraham watched me sympathetically. "The rain's stopping, anyway," he said.

Strether slapped me on the back. "It's part of the total experience," he said, and he sloshed ahead.

"Terns!" Hunt shouted, aiming a finger.

Up went nine pairs of binoculars—all except mine; I was busy splashing through mud toward hard ground.

Dr. Hurlburt counted aloud, "One, two . . . three blacks . . . and two common!"

"I knew the trip to McGonigal would be worth-while!" Strether exclaimed.

"Terns," Ingraham said, marking his card. "Did you see them, darling?" he asked his wife.

"Not really. We seem to be walking so fast."

Strether, if he noticed, paid no attention. "Terns!" he said, as if speaking to himself. "Didn't expect them this morning."

"Listen!" Mrs. Hurlburt called out, raising her hand. "A song sparrow." She said to me. "One of the songs I know by heart."

"Three more redwings," Miss Folger-Robinson called to Ingraham.

Hunt shouted, "I hear a killdeer up ahead." He paused, looking first at the remaining swampland around the pond, then at the beginning of the woods to our right.

Wide streaks of blue sky bordered the horizon to the east. The wind seemed drier. We had reached the edge of the woods. Strether and Hunt opened their map and leaned over it. I stopped to scrape mud from my shoes, then hastened to catch up with the others, arriving in time to see Hunt cock his head briefly, then report, "A bay-breasted warbler over there, hear it?"

I heard nothing.

"Our second warbler," Miss Folger-Robinson said.

"There it is again," Hunt said. "Mark it down, Ingraham."

"Could we track it down?" Mrs. Ingraham asked. "I've never seen a—"

She broke off. Strether and Hunt were gone. We started after them.

Mrs. Ingraham, I noticed, my heart skipping, held her hand pressed into the small of her back. She shifted Kathy, who seemed still to be looking up at the terns circling the pond.

"Could we walk just a little more slowly?" I shouted to Strether.

"Two catbirds!" Hunt called. He raised his hand for silence. "And I hear a yellow warbler. Got that, Ingraham?"

Dr. Hurlburt helped his wife across a huge puddle. "The yellow warbler was that *weet weet weet weet tsee tsee* sound, dear," he said.

Mrs. Hurlburt repeated the call. "I'll try to remember, dear," she said.

A raindrop slid under my collar and trickled down my neck. A branch lying unnoticed on the ground caught my foot and almost threw me. Underfoot, the path had turned to mud, which gathered heavily again on my shoes.

"Watch out for the branch," I called to the Ingrahams. If she has her child here, I thought, she can call it Robin.

Birding, indeed.

"Are you warm enough?" Ingraham asked his wife. "You ought to fasten your collar. It's still cool out."

Dutifully, Mrs. Ingraham fastened her jacket collar.

"Another yellow warbler," Hunt shouted. "Do you hear it?"

"How about *seeing* . . . ?" Mrs. Ingraham began.

I was not looking where I walked. A branch of box elder swinging upward scratched my throat and knocked my cap off. A heavy twig rolled away from under my feet. I sprawled flat on the muddy path.

Ahead of me Hunt called to Ingraham, "Two cardinals! And a yellow-throated vireo, hear it?"

"Wait!" Miss Folger-Robinson cried.

Rising, I started to assure her. "I'm all—"

She was not even looking at me. Instead she pointed to a clump of trees on a rise in the woods. "There in the beech tree, near the redbud," she called.

I saw the two Gnomes freeze to a stop. They raised their binoculars. Behind me, the Ingrahams and the Hurlburts, too, stood motionless, looking up at the beech tree.

"Where?" I asked. "Where? Where?"

Miss Folger-Robinson tiptoed back to me, turned me toward the right, and, raising her hand, she pointed to the top of the beech tree.

Blue sky, washed by the rain, glistened clean and clear through the woods. The fresh subtle green of the leaves shone transparent in the morning sunlight.

Miss Folger-Robinson said to me, "Look up higher."

A flash of red at the top of the beech tree caught my eyes. I raised my binoculars, searched anxiously through the tree, and picked up the tanager.

"Oh," I said. Its brilliant red feathers shone like velvet against the blue sky.

Mrs. Ingraham cried, "I see it!"

Afraid that if I breathed the tanager might move out of my field of vision, I held my binoculars steady. I whispered aloud, "Oh my gosh, my gosh."

The tanager fluttered its jet black wings and darted—a flash of scarlet in the sunlight—from the beech tree to the flowering redbud. "Oh my gosh," I repeated.

The two Gnomes lowered their binoculars, turned to me, and whispered, "Isn't it beautiful?"

"Beautiful, beautiful," I said.

They nodded knowingly, in unison, at me and at the Hurlburts, who stood beside me.

The sun warmed my face. The tanager hopped to the topmost branch of the flowering redbud, raised its head, and suddenly started to sing to the morning sun.

"Can you distinguish it?" Hunt said. "Like a robin with a sore throat."

But, my heart beating fast, I had been listening to something else, an imaginary sound beyond the song of the scarlet tanager outlined against the clear blue sky. I remembered something that had been said to me about a door opening. I lowered my binoculars; and indeed, there in front of me, watching me, stood Miss Folger-Robinson. She smiled, then moved her hand gently in the air, as if she were turning a knob.

"You see," she said to me.

IV

Listen, The Red-Eyed Vireo

Wendell Hunt had charge of today's bird walk.

"The theme this morning," he announced to the Olney Bird Watchers, as we gathered in the university gardens on the edge of the campus, "is bird *songs*. I'm going to tape the calls and the songs of some of the birds around us."

"Good heavens," Mrs. Hurlburt murmured.

I knew what she meant. For there in the midst of the beds of early June roses and young petunia plants, Hunt had scattered what appeared to be a formidable mass of recording equipment. Wires stretched from strange boxes topped with reels and buttons and dials to a huge dish-shaped, plastic reflector (the reflector seemed to me to be almost three feet in diameter) in which was fastened a microphone.

Miss Folger-Robinson and the Gnomes studied the equipment politely. Obviously they were baffled. "It looks like an enormous salad bowl," Miss Folger-Robinson commented.

Dr. Hurlburt attempted to be more co-operative. "There's the work that Allen and Kellogg did on songbirds at Cornell, of course," he said. "Fascinating study," he added, cheerfully.

"What's the range for sounds?" Strether asked, tapping the reflector.

At that moment an indigo bunting flashed past us. I saw Strether turn his head for just a second to watch it. The Gnomes started to raise their binoculars, and I cried out, "Indigo . . . !"

"*Sounds*," said Hunt loudly, so that the Olney Bird Watchers froze halfway in their movement, "sounds can be picked up by the parabolic reflector from a distance of about seventy-five feet." His voice precluded further interest in *seeing* any birds. He pointed to the microphone fixed inside the reflector. "The nerve center," he said, looking at us meaningfully. "It requires absolute quiet, except of course for the bird song it's trying to pick up."

Two workmen appeared outside the stadium across the road and shouted greetings to each other. Hunt frowned. One of the men climbed into a car and drove away, while the other, alone and silent, walked slowly toward the north stands. With a sigh of relief Hunt lifted the huge reflector and aimed it in the direction of the chattering of sparrows in the row of arborvitae bordering the gardens. The Gnomes stepped away from him uncertainly, as if he were about to explode.

I found myself watching Hunt nervously. He hurried toward the recording machine, pressed a switch, then, holding the reflector extended in front of him, he dashed toward the arborvitae until the reflector cord was drawn its full length. The reels on the recorder whirred. A red light glistened.

Miss Folger-Robinson said, "I hope that—"

"Hssst!" Strether warned.

Miss Folger-Robinson stopped short. Hunt glared. His lips

shaped a silent reproach. The reels on the recording machine turned. The sparrows chattered in the arborvitae. Hunt strained toward them, the reflector held high over his head. The Gnomes clung to each other. Mrs. Hurlburt, for just a few seconds, turned away, raised her binoculars, and scanned the nearby sycamore, searching perhaps for the indigo bunting.

"Dear . . ." Dr. Hurlburt whispered to her.

Hunt lowered the reflector, ran to the recording machine, frowned as he pushed some buttons, and then said, "Now for the playback. We'll see what we picked up."

Hesitantly, the Olney Bird Watchers approached. Hunt pushed a button. The reels on the recorder slipped, then began to turn. The Gnomes stepped back, watching the machine suspiciously. A raucous screech blared out over the gardens, filling the warm June morning. Hunt, kneeling beside the recorder, pushed a couple of buttons. The screeching sound became a whirring sound, and suddenly we heard Miss Folger-Robinson's recorded voice saying, "I hope that—" Then Strether's recorded "hssst!"

Miss Folger-Robinson and Strether looked at one another guiltily. For a few seconds we listened to the scratchy twittering of sparrows emerging from the recorder, then silence, and, as the reels turned again, Dr. Hurlburt's voice saying, "Dear . . ." Finally the whirring sound became a penetrating screech once again.

"Something's wrong," Hunt said, making a dive for a switch.

I sat down on the field-stone wall surrounding the pond in the gardens, while Hunt and Strether bent over the recorder, examining and testing dials. Strether perused a booklet of instructions. The Gnomes and the Hurlburts wandered closer to the sycamore tree, raised their binoculars, and scanned the branches. Miss Folger-Robinson sat down beside me, in the June sunlight. She nodded in Hunt's direction and whispered to me, "He's *mad* about *sounds*, isn't he?" Then, irrelevantly, "Wouldn't it be nice if the Ingrahams had a boy?" she said. "That's what they want."

Mrs. Ingraham had gone to the hospital, at last.

"It'll be sometime this morning," Miss Folger-Robinson said.

"A boy," I said, vaguely.

Mrs. Hurlburt called out, "We've found the indigo bunting!"

"There it is!" the Gnomes cried.

Hunt, ignoring them, hurried to his car, returned with a tool kit, and bent over the microphone attached to the reflector. "I've located the trouble," he shouted to us. "We'll be ready to try again in a minute."

"Oh dear," Mrs. Hurlburt said.

"Dear," Dr. Hurlburt said to her.

Mrs. Hurlburt patted his arm. "Yes, dear," she said. She looked around her at the trees and sky. "But on such a lovely June morning."

The reflector held high, Hunt approached the arborvitae, startling the Gnomes, who were still concentrating on the indigo bunting.

"Ready?" Hunt called to Strether.

Strether nodded, pressed a switch on the recording machine, and adjusted some dials. Hunt aimed the reflector. The reels on the recorder whirred. The red light gleamed. The Olney Bird Watchers held their breath.

After a few moments of silence, Hunt shouted to Strether, "Switch her off!"

Strether switched her off. Hunt signaled us to gather round. "Just to give you an idea of how effectively the sound can be collected," he said, excitedly.

He reversed the reels, then pressed still another button and stood back, smiling in anticipation.

We heard a whirring sound, then Miss Folger-Robinson's clear voice saying, "I hope that—" followed by Strether's "hssst!" and a moment later, Dr. Hurlburt's "dear . . ."

"Good grief," Hunt said to Strether, "I thought you'd erased the tape."

"I thought *you* had," Strether countered.

The Gnomes sighed.

Miss Folger-Robinson once again sat down beside me, on the wall. "*Seeing* birds is difficult anyway, now that the leaves are out on the trees," she said philosophically.

"It'll take only a minute," Hunt announced.

"So many wires and things," one of the Gnomes whispered.

"It's supposed to be a bird *walk*," her sister said.

Mrs. Hurlburt sighed, ignoring her husband's warning glance. "What I mean is," she said, "it's somehow like throwing away the Hershey bar and eating the wrapper."

"With almonds or without?" I asked, in an attempt at lightness. The sunlight glistened through the trees. I took off my jacket, rolled up my shirt sleeves, and gave myself over to the warmth of the morning.

Hunt's outcry startled me into wakefulness. "Listen!" he called. I looked up and saw him pointing toward the top of the sycamore tree, his face suddenly radiant. "Listen!" he repeated.

From the sycamore came the song of a bird, the sound rising sweet and clear above the miscellaneous twittering of sparrows. I squinted at the tree, trying to locate the bird through the thick leaves. The triple notes of the bird's song continued without a stop.

Strether and Dr. Hurlburt cried out, "A red-eyed vireo!"

I ruffled through Peterson's bird guide. Vireo, Red-eyed! I found it. "Well," I said.

The others had already trained their binoculars on the treetop.

"I can see something moving up there," Miss Folger-Robinson said, "but the leaves—"

Hunt cried excitedly, "That's the bird I'm after. I've heard it the past two mornings."

Dr. Hurlburt nodded, "I always say it sounds like a robin that's forgotten to stop singing."

"The tape!" Hunt shouted to Strether, waving at the recording machine. Strether lowered his binoculars and dove for the switch on the recorder. The tape had fallen off one of the reels. Strether fumbled with it.

"Good grief, I'll fix it!" Hunt cried, pushing at Strether's hands.

Both of them tugged at the reels, and after a moment of frantic groping they succeeded in fastening the tape.

"Now!" Hunt said, and made a dash for the reflector.

At the same moment the deafening roar of a jackhammer tore into the quiet of the June morning. His face stricken, Hunt stopped short. He gaped, unbelieving, toward the noise. In the football stadium across the road a jackhammer operator—the workman we had seen arriving—had begun his attack against concrete: outlined against the sky, he stood at the top row of the stadium in a cloud of concrete dust. I recalled reading in the student newspaper that a press box was to be built for the broadcasting of sports events.

"The vireo!" Hunt cried.

Strether started running toward the stadium. He called over his shoulder, "I'll get him to stop."

The Olney Bird Watchers strained to hear the song of the red-eyed vireo over the rat-tat-tat of the jackhammer. Miss Folger-Robinson reported, "I can't see any movement in the tree, at all."

"There!" the Gnomes cried.

"I still see him up there, but I can't hear him," Mrs. Hurlburt said.

A moment later, through our binoculars, we watched Strether join the jackhammer operator at the top of the stadium. Strether pointed in the direction of the sycamore tree. The bobbing of Strether's head and the sweep of his arm as he spoke to the operator indicated his earnestness. But the jackhammer continued to roar. The operator shrugged his shoulders.

"He isn't going to stop!" Hunt cried. He put down the reflector and raced toward the stadium.

"I'll be glad," Mrs. Hurlburt said, "when he finishes his thesis. All this worry about *sounds* . . ."

"Remember Allen and Kellogg at Cornell, dear," Dr. Hurlburt said.

"Yes, dear," Mrs. Hurlburt said.

Hunt's figure appeared at the top of the stadium. Once again the Olney Bird Watchers raised their binoculars. We could see Hunt talking excitedly. His arm swept the horizon and he pointed toward the sycamore tree, shaking his head. The jackhammer operator shook *his* head and turned away from Hunt. The roar of the jackhammer continued.

"No recording today," Miss Folger-Robinson said, delighted. The six of us exchanged glances that indicated our relief: perhaps now we could go on a walk during which we could *see* birds.

"We might even get some warblers," Mrs. Hurlburt said.

"Miss Billings reported a prothonotary down at Wander Creek," Miss Folger-Robinson said.

As Hunt and Strether returned I stepped back from the others, aware that, huddled together as we were, we must have seemed almost conspiratorial; and all at once I felt sorry for Hunt. He did not speak. Crestfallen, solemn, he started to gather together his recording equipment.

Strether shook his head. "We couldn't budge him," he said, nodding in the direction of the stadium and the roar of the jackhammer against concrete.

For just a moment, as the noise subsided briefly—the jackham-

mer operator shifted his position—we could hear the red-eyed vireo still singing madly at the top of the sycamore tree. The parabolic reflector in his hand, Hunt paused, listening to the song. Then the jackhammer roared again.

Mrs. Hurlburt said lightly, "Well, perhaps we can try recording some other day."

Miss Folger-Robinson and the Gnomes clucked sympathetically. "There's plenty of time for your thesis," Miss Folger-Robinson said; and the Gnomes echoed, "Time . . ."

Hunt faced the ladies. "I wasn't doing this for my thesis," he said. He shrugged. "I wanted to record the red-eyed vireo's song and send it to the hospital, to Mrs. Ingraham, as a present from the Olney Bird Watchers." And he added, "I thought it might cheer her up."

Motionless, the Olney Bird Watchers stared at Hunt. The noise of the jackhammer rattled through the June air. The indigo bunting darted past, but no one turned to look at it. Mrs. Hurlburt had dropped her kerchief, and now it fluttered to the ground, unheeded.

Mrs. Hurlburt said, slowly, "This isn't for your thesis?"

Dr. Hurlburt picked up her kerchief and handed it to her. He pressed her hand tenderly.

Miss Folger-Robinson tucked a strand of hair under her broad-brimmed hat. "I thought . . ." she said.

Hunt shook his head. "I just thought it would be fun to let the baby hear a bird song as soon as possible. And the red-eyed vireo's song is so beautiful. I felt the Ingrahams would be pleased." He started to wind wires around the recording machine.

I said haltingly, "Perhaps if we wait a while . . ."

Hunt shrugged again. "He's going to be working all morning. He refuses to stop."

"Wait!" Miss Folger-Robinson said. She cupped her ear and stepped toward the sycamore tree, listening; then she nodded. "The vireo's still there," she said. "Now, then," she turned to Hunt, "how much time do you think you'll need? I mean," she said, as she waved in the direction of the jackhammer roar, "how long do you want that thing turned off?"

Hunt raised his eyebrows. "Ten minutes," he said.

Miss Folger-Robinson looked thoughtful, then nodded emphatically. "Ten minutes," she said. "You shall have them!"

"He won't stop work, he told us so," Strether repeated.

Miss Folger-Robinson smiled, almost wickedly. "Do you remember," she asked, "when the farmer out on Collins Road came after us for trespassing?"

For a moment the Olney Bird Watchers stared at Miss Folger-Robinson; then they, too, began to smile, almost wickedly.

Hunt chuckled.

"Perfect," Strether said.

"Oh dear," the Gnomes said.

"What happened?" I asked. "That was before my—"

"Exactly," Miss Folger-Robinson said to me. "Come along with us. You can help."

"Help *what?*" I asked.

Miss Folger-Robinson had taken each of the Gnomes by the arm, and now the three women started toward the stadium. "Just come along," Miss Folger-Robinson called to me.

"But I don't know what . . ." I said, trotting after them. As I looked back I saw Hunt confidently setting up his recording machine again. The innocence of the early June roses and the newly transplanted petunias in the gardens were, I thought, in strange contrast to the determination and intrigue that emanated from the three ladies hurrying toward the stadium.

"Ladies!" I called.

But Miss Folger-Robinson and the Gnomes were busy whispering to each other. Only after they had crossed the football field and started up the concrete steps of the stadium did they turn and wait for me.

"It's a lovely morning," Miss Folger-Robinson shouted to me, above the noise of the jackhammer.

"Lovely," the Gnomes echoed, nodding and smiling.

The jackhammer operator, without stopping his work, eyed us warily as we approached. He wore a green visored baseball cap pulled low on his forehead, shielding his face from the sun. Now that I was close to him, I saw the startling tattoo on his arm: a buxom nude shimmying in rhythm with the rapid pounding of the jackhammer he held. The Gnomes pretended not to notice; they continued nodding and smiling.

Miss Folger-Robinson lifted her hand in a friendly greeting. The man operating the jackhammer nodded briefly, his jaw set. Miss Folger-Robinson shouted to him, "It's a lovely morning." She pointed toward the binoculars around her neck, then let her hand cover the landscape with a wide sweeping gesture while her lips formed the words, "Bird watching."

The operator, in a cloud of concrete dust, nodded again, shifted, and braced himself against the slamming action of the jackhammer. Clinging to each other, the Gnomes walked cautiously along the topmost bench in the stadium, only pretending to be looking out toward the distant trees and the flight of a pair of mourning doves. When they were close to the jackhammer operator, they climbed down from the bench into the aisle, clutched at the parapet, and peered at the ground far below them.

Suddenly one of them stepped backward, raised her hand to her forehead, and with a low moan sank onto the bench—in spite of my fright, I was reminded of the heroine in a silent movie. The other sister cried out, "Fainted . . . her heart . . . !" Miss Folger-Robinson screamed. The jackhammer operator stopped drilling and whirled around.

Good heavens! I thought.

Trembling, I seized the hand of the prostrate Gnome—she was stretched out full-length on the bench, her eyes closed tightly—

and I began to rub her wrist. The jackhammer operator stared at us, aghast. Miss Folger-Robinson cried out, "She fainted! Heart . . ." She began to rub the Gnome's other wrist.

The second Gnome waved her hands in the air and repeated, "Fainted . . . fainted . . . oh . . . !"

"Get a doctor!" the jackhammer operator shouted, swept up into the drama at last.

Miss Folger-Robinson put her arm under the Gnome's shoulders and attempted to lift her. "I can't pick her up," she said, weakly.

"Fainted . . . fainted . . . !" the other Gnome cried.

"Let me try," I said.

Miss Folger-Robinson pushed me away, rather gently. "You'll need help."

"Let me!" the jackhammer operator cried.

"Please do," Miss Folger-Robinson said. I saw her glance at her watch as she stepped back to make room for the jackhammer operator. She said quickly, "But we have to let her rest for just a few minutes. Moving her now may . . ." She shook her head at the dire consequences.

"Keep rubbin' her wrists . . . the circulation going," the jackhammer operator ordered in a loud voice. He pushed Miss Folger-Robinson aside, picked up the Gnome's hand, and started to chafe her wrist. He looked down at the figure tattooed on his arm and modestly lowered the sleeve of his denim shirt.

"Fainted . . . fainted . . . !" the other Gnome continued to cry.

"How pale she is!" Miss Folger-Robinson wailed.

I stared at the woman stretched out on the bench—she did not seem *that* pale to me—and then I stared at Miss Folger-Robinson. Miss Folger-Robinson looked away hurriedly. She raised her hand to brush back a stray strand of hair, and as she did so, she glanced again at her wrist watch. "To the doctor's!" she cried. "If you two men lift her now . . . carefully . . ."

The helpless twittering of the women continued during the slow, slow descent down the stadium steps. "Don't jiggle her!" Miss Folger-Robinson cried, stopping us from time to time.

"Fainted . . . fainted . . . !" the second Gnome wailed.

The jackhammer operator shouted to me, "I think I'd manage better carryin' her by myself."

Miss Folger-Robinson touched me on the shoulder. "Let him

carry her." She smiled at the man who struggled with his burden. "What," she asked, "would we have done without you?" Her voice was shamelessly flattering.

We had reached the bottom of the stairs. "Across here," Miss Folger-Robinson directed, leading the way across the football field. Her car stood in front of the university gardens. She hurried ahead and opened the door. "In here!"

The Gnome was deposited, with care, on the back seat. She moaned an unnecessarily prolonged "ohh . . ."

Miss Folger-Robinson turned away from the frown I directed at her. She shook hands with the jackhammer operator, thanking him, leading him away from the car. ". . . wonderful help," I heard her say.

"D'yuh want me to drive yuh to the doctor?" the jackhammer operator asked.

Miss Folger-Robinson assured him that would not be necessary. "You must be anxious to get back to your drilling," she said. As a second prolonged "ohh . . ." drifted from the back seat of the car, Miss Folger-Robinson added, "Good-by. Thanks again," this time giving him a decisive push.

The jackhammer operator, obviously filled with the satisfaction of a magnanimous job well done, strode to the stadium and disappeared behind the north stands.

"He's gone," Miss Folger-Robinson announced, poking her head inside the car.

The Gnome sat up. "Was I all right?" she asked.

"Splendid," her sister said, smiling. "Even better than last time."

"Ladies," I said. "Shameless!"

"Nonsense," Miss Folger-Robinson said. "Hunt got his ten minutes, didn't he? You did very well—just the right degree of concern," she added, touching my arm. "Now let's go hear what Hunt recorded."

The three women hurried back to the gardens, while I trailed behind them. The Olney Bird Watchers, gathered around Hunt, greeted us with a round of applause.

"It was perfect!" Strether announced.

"I got it!" Hunt said, beaming. "Listen!"

He started the tape, adjusted a dial, and stood back. The cheerful song of the red-eyed vireo flooded the morning.

Mrs. Hurlburt said, "It's the sweetest idea I ever heard of."

Suddenly the sound of the jackhammer ripped through the air. Hunt patted the recording machine. "He can tear down the whole stadium now, for all I care."

At the cry "Hey, there!" we turned, in a group, toward the road. Ingraham came running across the garden, his face aglow behind his horn-rims. He called out, "It's a boy! Seven pounds two ounces! It's a boy!"

"A boy!" Miss Folger-Robinson and Mrs. Hurlburt cried.

"A boy!" the Gnomes echoed.

Hunt patted the recording machine again. Ingraham, catching his breath, shook hands with each of us. "Lydia's fine, though she's sorry she had to miss the bird walk today. And the boy's fine." He seemed, for the first time, to notice the recording equipment. "This looks interesting," he said. "Have you been able to record anything good? Too bad that jackhammer's making so much noise."

"Oh, we got something good," Hunt said, casually.

"You'll see," Strether said, smiling.

The Gnomes nodded. I found myself nodding, too. Miss Folger-Robinson patted Mr. Ingraham's arm.

The Hurlburts said, "You'll see."

"Fine," Ingraham said.

"A boy," he repeated, his voice filled with wonder. "Seven pounds two ounces. I just wanted you to know." He started to walk away, then hesitantly turned and faced us again. He grinned. "By the way," he said, "we think we have a perfect name for him, all things considered."

It can't be, I thought.

The Olney Bird Watchers leaned forward, waiting.

Ingraham's grin broadened. "Robin," he said proudly. "We're going to call him Robin."

V

A Walk in Truro

"Here we go!" the Gnomes said brightly to Miss Folger-Robinson and me, and the four of us, bedecked with binoculars, stepped out of the house into the wet gray afternoon in Truro. Heavy rain had fallen steadily since my arrival on Cape Cod, the previous night.

Miss Folger-Robinson raised her hand, testing the weather. "It's stopping," she said, and she sloshed across the wet lawn.

I drew my cap down over my eyes to protect my glasses from the downpour. At the same time I buttoned the collar of my field jacket to ward off the surprising chill in the salt air. *My first day in Truro!* I thought, sloshing after Miss Folger-Robinson. The gloom of the August afternoon pressed down upon the wide marsh across the road and the hills of scrub pine all around me. The sky, the Pamet River, the weathered shingle houses on the Truro moors—everything was gray, dripping with rain.

"We're a mile from the ocean and two miles from the bay," Miss Folger-Robinson said.

In spite of the protection of my cap, rain blurred my glasses. I said, looking back longingly at the house, "The birds won't have much color today."

"Herring gull over the marsh," the Gnomes called to me.

I looked up at the large gull sailing toward the distant hills and I caught the slanting rain full on my face. One of the Gnomes disappeared in the garage and emerged a moment later tugging a child's wagon, hurrying to catch up with us. "For beach plums," she explained.

"The beach plums are ripe," Miss Folger-Robinson said.

"Of course," I said, shaking rain from my cap.

We started down the road in single file, Miss Folger-Robinson striding ahead first, and the Gnomes following, pulling the wagon. Disconsolately I trailed after the three women. I looked around, baffled by Truro. Where was the friendly Cape Cod town I had envisaged when Miss Folger-Robinson and the Gnomes had sent me a letter, urging me to visit them in the summer home they shared? I had never before been to the Cape; my images of it came from the novels of Joseph C. Lincoln and Sara Ware Bassett, novels I started to read as soon as I accepted the invitation.

Where, then, were the white picket fences, the elm-lined streets, the fishing boats and wharves? Where were the kindly, industrious natives who said "calc'late," and where were the hillocks of sand called dunes? I had expected to be surrounded by the sea, everywhere on the Cape. Something was wrong. Truro was country; it was moors and low hills covered with scrub pine. But no sea.

Behind us, from what Miss Folger-Robinson called Cemetery Hill, the chimes of the town hall rang out the quarter hour. Even the sound of the chimes seemed wet in the dismal afternoon. Rain beat down upon us. The gusts of wind from the east were cold, filled with the taste of salt. I wrapped my handkerchief around the lenses of my binoculars, hoping to keep them dry.

"There'll be kelp on the shore," Miss Folger-Robinson called back to me, enthusiastically. Rain dripped from the brim of her hat.

The Gnomes, with a whispered warning to me, stopped short in the middle of the road, pointing toward the marsh that bordered the narrow Pamet River. "Look!" Miss Folger-Robinson halted abruptly. I squinted at the marsh, trying to pick out some movement, but the rain on my glasses made a blur of Truro.

"I see them," Miss Folger-Robinson nodded. "Next to the clump of cattails." She pointed. "Down at the edge of the stream. See them? Yellowlegs."

I saw them, dimly, wetly.

"Are they lesser or greater, can you tell?" Miss Folger-Robinson asked. She clapped her hands, and the yellowlegs, startled, rose from the marsh with a whistling sound, *whew, whew, whew.*

"That's the call of the greater," Miss Folger-Robinson said, satisfied.

The Gnomes, their heads tilted listening to the cry of the birds, nodded in agreement. "Greater," they said.

"Greater," I echoed; and as we plowed on through the rain I made a mental note to study Richard Pough on the distinctive calls of the greater and lesser yellowlegs.

The wagon bounced along the road, wheels creaking. Miss Folger-Robinson and the Gnomes continued to scan the marsh and the cheerless sky. I sniffed at the rain and the salt air and the . . . what was it? I wondered.

The Gnomes saw me. "It's bayberry that you smell," one of them said; and then, without warning, they hurried ahead a few yards tugging the wagon behind them. "Beach plums!" they called, beckoning to me.

Miss Folger-Robinson had already trotted after them. She picked a handful of beach plums from the bush beside the road and held them out to me. "Taste one," she said. "They're really wonderful."

"They look so—miniature," I said. I took a plum from Miss Folger-Robinson and tasted it. The flavor was miniature; and the plum pit, when I held it between my fingers, was an exquisite miniature of a plum pit.

"Delicious," the Gnomes said, happily.

I could hear the rain dripping down through the scrub pine on top of the high banks that lined the road. I reached out to pick a couple of beach plums, and rain from the leaves of the bush drenched my hand.

"They make wonderful jelly," Miss Folger-Robinson said. She concentrated on picking. With the Gnomes leading we edged our way slowly down the road, dropping handfuls of beach plums into the wagon.

The chimes in the town hall struck again, and the notes, slightly out of tune, echoed in the air; then the sound settled into the low hills of scrub pine, and I heard only the patter of rain on the beach-plum bushes and Miss Folger-Robinson's tuneless humming.

"Another herring gull overhead," one of the Gnomes said.

I pretended to be busy gathering beach plums. Then I heard the lonely complaining cry of the sea gull. I emptied a handful of beach plums into the wagon and looked up to see the gull flapping its solitary way toward the sea. Suddenly the desolation and loneliness of the marsh and the hills of Truro overwhelmed me: whatever had Miss Folger-Robinson and the Gnomes seen in this place, in the gray wet dreariness, in the lonely gull gliding against the gray sky?

I brushed the rain from my face. The handkerchief I had wrapped around my binoculars was soaked. Sighing, I put the handkerchief into my pocket and slipped my binoculars under my jacket in an attempt to keep them dry.

"It's a fine day for sea gulls," I said, shaking the rain off my cap.

"The rain in Truro is so *soft,*" Miss Folger-Robinson said, dropping some beach plums into the wagon.

And so wet, I thought; but I only nodded.

"We needn't stay out long this afternoon," Miss Folger-Robinson said, shaking rain from her hat. I nodded, more vigorously.

"I'd like to get some kelp on the shore," Miss Folger-Robinson added.

"Kelp," the Gnomes said.

But I only half listened to the ladies. We were approaching a bend in the road, and now a new sound, more insistent than the dripping of the rain, intruded. I strained, trying to place it; and for the first time since I had arrived on the Cape—I had been in Truro almost twenty-four hours—I realized that I was listening to the sea beating against the shore in the distance.

I walked ahead more quickly than the others; and as I came to the bend I caught my first glimpse of the ocean at Truro through a low dip between the dunes. Gray, chill, almost forbidding, the line of white-capped breakers bore down upon the shore.

Miss Folger-Robinson and the Gnomes stopped beside me and looked at the sea. "You'll find that no matter how many times you see it . . ." Miss Folger-Robinson said gently; but she did not finish.

"Splendid," the Gnomes said, just as gently.

"The beach is so empty," I said, thinking of the wharves and the fishing boats I had expected, of paved streets leading down to the sea.

Miss Folger-Robinson nodded. All she said was, "Truro takes a little time, wait and see."

We left the wagon at the side of the road and began to plod

through the wet sand that led through the dunes onto the beach. No hillocks these! The sand dunes, covered with beach grass waving in the cold wind, towered a hundred feet above me. We passed through the cut in the dunes, and I stared, awed, at the enormous hills of sand that sloped down to meet the shore. The beach, extending north and south as far as I could see, was empty. No one. A flock of small birds scurried along the wet sand, pushing close to the edge of the sea in the ebb of each wave, retreating with quick comic steps as a new wave broke over the shore.

"Sanderlings and semipalmated sandpipers," Miss Folger-Robinson called to me.

Shivering in the chill salt air directly off the sea, I felt the loneliness of the wide empty beach and the wet slopes of the dunes. I listened to the beating of the surf.

As we stepped forward onto the beach the sanderlings and sandpipers scampered away from us, rose suddenly in a flurry of wingbeats, flashed over a wave, and fluttered down the wet strand. The high plaintive cry the birds made in flight added to the desolation of Truro. I felt wet sand slipping into my shoes.

Miss Folger-Robinson said, pointing, "The sanderling is the one with the distinctive white stripe on its wings." She drew a white stripe in the air. "The others are semipals. They're new birds for your life list, aren't they?" And she added, brightly, "Well, expand your bird watching! Expand your bird watching!" This time her hand swept the air to indicate all the Cape.

The Gnomes gathered pieces of wet kelp from the edge of the sea; they selected the kelp they wanted and stuffed it into their jacket pockets. I tried to dry my glasses with my handkerchief but succeeded only in smearing them. "It's hard to see this afternoon," I said, shielding my eyes against the rain.

I drew my binoculars from the protection of my jacket and, scanning the beach, picked up the flock of sandpipers and sanderlings. But by the time I had focused properly the birds had scurried from my field of vision. I lowered my binoculars, located the flock farther down the beach, and picked them up again in my field glasses. The flock ran along the shore, heads bobbing constantly, searching for food, beaks digging into the edge of each wave that swept up onto the sand. On the perimeter of the flock scurried two brownish birds, larger than the others, with long, almost needlelike bills.

"Snipe!" I cried, determined to show some enthusiasm.

The Gnomes raised their binoculars. "Dowitchers!" they said, smiling.

"Isn't that a wonderful name for a shore bird?" Miss Folger-Robinson said.

At that moment the Gnomes, gesturing excitedly, broke into a trot down the beach. *To catch the dowitchers?* I wondered, startled.

"Cable reel!" they cried.

Apparently Miss Folger-Robinson understood, for she began to run too. My shoes were full of sand, and I could only hobble after the three women, who stood now as close to the edge of the sea as the wash of waves permitted. The Gnomes began to unlace their sneakers, preparing to wade into the water. I saw what they were after: a large wooden reel on which a heavy cable had once been wound. The words "Acme Cable Company, Brooklyn, New York" were printed on the side of the reel in bright yellow letters.

"I'll get it!" I cried. Following in the wake of a receding wave I ran down the strand, toward the reel. My feet sank into the soft wet sand, but I plowed forward, seized the huge wooden reel from the edge of a new wave, and tried to haul it onto the shore. Miss Folger-Robinson and the Gnomes called out a warning. A second wave, filled with breath-taking vigor and wetness, caught me and pushed the cable and me onto the shore. I stumbled, almost falling flat. Icy water swirled over my knees. With one hand I clung to the reel and with the other hand I held my binoculars in the air. The Gnomes grabbed the cable reel and Miss Folger-Robinson grabbed me.

"Good heavens," I said. I gasped again as the cold wind whipped my drenched trousers against my legs.

"Are you all right?" Miss Folger-Robinson and the Gnomes asked, anxiously.

Rain pelted me. I realized that I was still holding my binoculars high in the air.

"We'd better get you home," Miss Folger-Robinson said.

I wrung water out of the cuffs of my trousers. The sand in my shoes had turned to mud. I limped across the beach, sat down on the edge of the wet road, and emptied mud from my shoes. We started home at a half run, the Gnomes pulling the wagon in which the beach plums rattled, Miss Folger-Robinson and I together pushing the large wooden cable reel before us. A car coming down the road swerved to avoid us. I saw the surprised look on the driver's face. As he turned to watch us, he almost missed the curve in the road and I found myself waving to him wildly, to signal him. He waved back, still surprised; then he turned quickly, and with a screeching of tires rounded the bend.

That evening, as I stood before the pine logs burning in the fireplace—a fire in August!—I listened to the rain beating against the window, and for a moment I experienced again the icy wet chill I had felt on the beach as the wave swirled round me. The cable reel, transformed now into a coffee table in front of the sofa, had on it a candle stuck into a cork float onto which Miss Folger-Robinson had glued some sea shells. I could hear the Gnomes moving about in the kitchen, washing glass jars for the jelly they were making. The sweet smell of the beach plums cooking on the stove seeped into the living room.

I sat down on the sofa, and, using the flat surface of the cable reel, I addressed picture post cards to Strether, Hunt, the Ingrahams, and the Hurlburts. I wrote them that I was having a wonderful time, that I had seen sandpipers and dowitchers, and that I was certainly expanding my life list of birds. But all the time I listened to the rain sweeping down against the house.

Miss Folger-Robinson, working at the desk in the far corner of the living room, cautiously lifted a piece of paper from a small square of glass, watching to see that the kelp had transferred from the glass to the paper. She came toward me triumphantly.

"Doesn't it make a beautiful design?" she said, holding the paper out for me to see.

It was true: the kelp pressed onto the paper formed a delicate, lacey pattern, like a fine etching.

Miss Folger-Robinson said, "All I have to do now is draw a border around the kelp, fold the paper, and I have an attractive Christmas card."

I sneezed, twice. "You ought to sketch in a few lines in one corner, to represent a sea gull," I said.

"Splendid idea!" Miss Folger-Robinson exclaimed, and she went into the kitchen to tell the Gnomes.

I listened once again to the rain beating down on the house; then I walked to the window and peered out into the vast blackness of the Cape. Rain trickled down the windowpane. I sneezed again.

Truro, I thought: what am I doing here, anyway?

But the next morning the sun was shining. The brightness of the light that poured into my bedroom window woke me. I opened my eyes to a cloudless blue-washed sky. The Pamet River marsh and the low hills around Truro glistened, silvery green in the clear sunlight.

For a couple of moments I listened to the silence of the house; then quietly I got out of bed, dressed, picked up my binoculars from the bureau, slipped Peterson into my jacket pocket, and I tiptoed outdoors, closing the screen door behind me so that it made no sound. Standing at the edge of the road, I surveyed the Pamet River marsh, which glistened in the sun: I looked westward toward the bay and eastward toward the sea; and I decided, after a moment, to walk to the sea. It isn't every day a man can walk to the ocean, I thought.

The early morning sun warmed me. As I started down the road, which was already dry, I threw open my jacket. The gray and white Cape Cod houses scattered on the distant dunes gleamed in the sunshine. The narrow Pamet glistened. A breeze stirred the tall cattails in the salt marsh. From Cemetery Hill, back in the direction of Route 6, came the off-key tolling of the town-hall chimes, striking the hour. The ringing of bells hung in the air, suspended in the scrub pine that covered the hills. Slowly the notes faded into silence.

I picked a few ripe beach plums and ate them for my breakfast. Over the Pamet I saw a pair of birds in flight, a markedly white stripe across their wings. I focused my binoculars on the birds:

sanderlings, on their way from the bay to the ocean. I felt the quick uplift of pleasure related to the identification of a species of bird, newly learned. The sanderlings skimmed the narrow river, dipped once to circle a cluster of cattails, and then disappeared around the bend.

In the warm sunshine I paused to listen: in the distance I heard the sound of the surf, somehow a familiar sound this morning. I walked quickly toward the bend in the road, and there before me, shimmering in the sunlight, lay the bright blue sea. That glimpse of the ocean, along with the Pamet River marsh and the hills of scrub pine, suddenly comprised all the world that existed, quiet, gentle. I took a deep breath of the clean salt air and of—I knew it now—bayberry. With that breath, something brushed me; I looked around me, my heart beating: that something was a new awareness of the peace and solitude of Truro.

Glorious, glorious, I thought.

As I hurried down the road toward the sea I held my hands open and caught the sunlight in them. This time I did not walk through the cut in the dunes in order to get to the shore. Instead I started to climb the highest dune, careful not to step on the beach grass that held the sand in place. At the top of the dune I surveyed the sea and paused to catch my breath. The wide beach, golden-yellow, stretched away on each side of me. Everywhere, everywhere, the sun, its light clear and warm, beat down upon the sea and sand and sky and me.

Overhead, a herring gull glided, like an odd-shaped gray-and-white kite against the clean blue sky. "Move over, mister," I said to the gull.

I removed my shoes and socks and planted my feet in the warm sand on the top of the dune. The sea, a sweep of sparkling blue water, met the broad horizon in a sharp line that I felt I could reach out and touch. Sea and sand and sky and me. Nothing else existed.

I shielded my eyes. No, I had been wrong: for there on the shore stood Miss Folger-Robinson and the Gnomes, their binoculars trained on a flock of birds that scurried down the beach.

Glorious, glorious, I thought again.

I called out to the three women. They looked up, saw me, and waved. My heart singing, my binoculars ready, I ran barefoot, breathlessly, down the steep slope of the dune, to join them.

VI

The Woman Who Fed Birds

On the second Saturday in October somewhere in the world a missile was hurled into space on a journey to the moon; and on the same Saturday the Olney Bird Watchers went on a bird walk. In the early dawn hung the first trace of a fall frost. The leaves in the maples had begun to turn yellow and red. As I dressed I listened to the babel of bird sounds outside my apartment window: the cooing of mourning doves, the bright whistle of a pair of cardinals, and the chatter of starlings; and I thought that the sounds had in them an edge of anxiety, an apprehension of months of cold weather ahead.

Across the street the young newsboy who delivered the morning paper at the Delta Chi House ran across the lawn, catching at his breath which steamed in the air in front of him. Then he leaped onto his bicycle and rode off.

I slung my binoculars over my shoulder, wound a wool scarf around my throat, and checked the pocket of my field jacket to be sure I had Peterson. I started up the street, my footsteps echoing in the clear cold air. I kicked at the red and yellow leaves lying on the sidewalk. The early morning air smelled of ripening apples.

A male cardinal, bright red in the morning sunlight, darted from Miss Folger-Robinson's redbud tree and swooped down onto the sidewalk, directly in front of me. He flitted nervously a short distance up the street, turned to watch me until I neared him, then he flew ahead of me once more, and waited. All the way to Upham Hall, where the Olney Bird Watchers were meeting, the bright red bird fluttered just ahead of me, flying from tree to tree, whistling full throatedly or making its short chipping sound.

The Gnomes were the first to see the cardinal and me crossing the campus. They waved to me; then I saw them pat each other on the arm and point to the cardinal. They called to the other bird watchers. Strether stopped talking to Mr. Hunt and the Hurlburts; they all turned to watch the cardinal as the bird fluttered into the low branches of the sycamore next to Upham Hall. Miss Folger-Robinson and the Ingrahams had already raised their binoculars. Leaning forward, the Olney Bird Watchers focused on the friendly cardinal. I could see their breath in the frosty air.

"I'm here," I said. No one paid any attention. The bird watchers continued to study the cardinal, which flashed brilliantly red in the morning sunlight.

Lowering her binoculars, Miss Folger-Robinson rummaged in the pocket of her jacket. She raised her hand and held out some sunflower seed to the cardinal. "Tzip, tzip! tzip, tzip!" she called, trying to attract its attention.

And suddenly I remembered Old Miss Simons, from way back in my boyhood. It had been years since I had thought of her. In that instant I saw her again, clearly. . . .

Old Miss Simons was the first person I ever knew who was interested in birds. Everyone in the neighborhood thought she was crazy because she fed sparrows and blue jays. At school—I was fourteen years old then—fellows like Al Goodwin and Howie Sands used to tap their foreheads meaningfully and say they had even heard Old Miss Simons *talking* to birds. The younger kids thought her big, old, brown-shingled house was haunted, and they hurried past the gate and the black iron fence that bordered the sidewalk.

I met Old Miss Simons late one October afternoon on my way home from the library, after school. As always, when I passed her house, I stared with fear and fascination at the dingy brown shingles, at the front porch covered with twisted wisteria vines, and I wondered if I would catch a glimpse of the old woman wandering among the trees in her yard, feeding birds.

Suddenly I heard a tapping at a window. My heart beating fast, I stopped to listen. The wisteria vines darkened the house, even in the bright fall sunshine. I located the tapping: it came from a window to the left of the front door. Behind the window a dark figure moved—Old Miss Simons, gesturing to me. While I stood there on the sidewalk gaping, the tapping stopped, the figure vanished from the window, and the only sound in the afternoon was the scolding of a blue jay in one of the maple trees in the yard. Then the front door opened, and Old Miss Simons stepped onto the porch.

She was tall, thin, white-haired; she stood very straight. As she walked slowly to the head of the porch steps she held up her hand and beckoned to me. "You!" she called. "You!"

For a couple of seconds I thought I would pretend I had not heard her. The blue jay, still scolding, darted out of the maple tree and flew into the thick rhododendron that grew along the iron fence. Old Miss Simons leaned against the porch post, waiting, but she did not call to me again.

She knew I had heard her. Hesitantly I put my hand on the iron gate and tried to open it. The gate was locked. Old Miss Simons' hand moved downward in the air, showing me what to do. "Push down on the handle," she said.

I pushed down on the handle, opened the gate, and took a few tentative steps toward the porch, leaving the gate ajar behind me. To avoid gaping at old Miss Simons, I stared at the wisteria that covered the porch—the leaves were dry and brown; they had already begun to fall from the vines.

Now that I was closer I noticed that Old Miss Simons looked sick. She nodded at me, then said, "Will you go on an errand . . . ?" I had to lean forward to hear what she said. "Will you go to the store for me?" she asked, blinking at me.

I could not trust myself to speak. I nodded in reply to her question.

Old Miss Simons groped in the pocket of her dress, and at last she held out a dollar bill. "Half a pound of ground beef and a pound of carrots," she said.

Careful not to touch her hand, I took the dollar from her. I repeated shakily, "Half a pound of ground beef and a pound of carrots." For a second I dared to stare at her. Her face was wrinkled. I hurried away from the house, and with a touch of excitement, all the way to the A & P on Belmont Avenue I kept telling myself, *I'm on an errand for Old Miss Simons . . .*

On the way back I clutched the groceries and the change from the dollar and finally I broke into a run, curious to see Old Miss Simons again. She sat in the sunlight on the top step of the porch. Her hands lay folded in her lap. Her head was raised so that her face caught the warm October afternoon sunshine.

She looked to me as if she were dying.

The iron gate squeaked as I pushed it open, and Old Miss Simons looked down from the porch and stared at me, trying, perhaps, to remember who I was. Her eyes were a deep blue. I said awkwardly, "I bought what you wanted me to," and I placed the bag of groceries on the step, beside her. I put the change from the dollar in her hand. Her fingers were long and thin.

Old Miss Simons glanced at the change, then she held out a dime to me. I told her that I did not want any money for the errand, but she did not hear me. She pressed the dime into my hand.

Suddenly a couple of blue jays, screeching, darted past the front porch and swooped into the rhododendron. Their cry startled me. I felt my heart beating fast again.

Old Miss Simons turned her head and listened to the scolding of the blue jays. She said quietly, "The feeders must be empty." She looked over her shoulder at a large yellow-and-black box of sunflower seed that stood beside the front door. I could see her trying to decide what to do.

After a moment she turned to me. She hesitated, as if she were building up energy to speak; then she said, "If you have time could you fill the bird feeders for me? The sunflower seed is in the box, there by the door. It won't take you long."

She spoke with a finality that left me no choice. Frightened, I climbed the porch steps, picked up the box of sunflower seed, and asked her, "How much do I use?"

"Just fill the feeders on the trees at that side of the house." She pointed.

Anxious to be finished, I hurried around the house. Half a dozen bird feeders, fashioned out of rough pine slabs, had been nailed to the trunks of the maples. Five birdbaths were set among the trees. At the moment the water in the birdbaths was dirty with twigs, dead leaves, bird droppings, and algae.

I emptied handfuls of sunflower seed into the feeders, heaping them until some of the seeds tumbled onto the ground. I found a watering can hanging on the spigot at the side of the house, and I emptied the birdbaths, rinsed them, and then filled them with clean water. All the sparrows in the neighborhood seemed to have followed me into the yard. I stopped to watch them. The sparrows crowded into the feeders, pecking at the sunflower seed, scattering it onto the ground where other sparrows fluttered nervously. A blue jay flew past me and swooped onto one of the feeders, routing the sparrows.

I walked back to the porch. Her eyes closed once more, Old Miss Simons sat on the steps, her thin face, pale, raised to the sun, her hands quiet in her lap. As I approached she waked and blinked at me as if she had forgotten me again. She dropped the change I had given her. I picked it up and put it in her lap.

"The birds are already eating," I said.

"Is the cardinal there?" Old Miss Simons asked me.

I told her I had seen only sparrows and a blue jay.

"The sparrows and the blue jays," Old Miss Simons said. She raised her shoulders. "Someone has to feed them." She spread her fingers, resting them on her knees. "How wonderful to be warm again at this time of year." Then, as if she were talking to herself, she added, "Sometimes I think the most wonderful thing is to feel the sun on your hands."

"Well, good-by," I said, and turned away.

Old Miss Simons said simply, "Come back tomorrow afternoon to take care of the feeders."

I did not answer her. I pushed open the gate and, once on the sidewalk, I hurried away. When I glanced back I saw Old Miss Simons sitting motionless in front of her house, in the afternoon sunlight that fell on the porch steps.

On my way to school in the morning, I stopped at Old Miss Simons' just long enough to peer through the fence at a flock of sparrows fluttering around the bird feeders, scattering sunflower seed. A blue jay shrieked a protest from its perch on the edge of a birdbath, then it flew upward into one of the feeders.

Howie Sands came running down the street on his way to school; he stopped beside me. "What're you looking at? Is Old Miss Simons there?" He was disappointed to see no one in the yard. "She's crazy," he said. He nudged me, started to walk away, then turned, waiting for me. "Hey, you're going to be late."

That afternoon, instead of going home after school, I walked over to the library across the street and sat alone at one of the long oak tables, ruffling through *The Saturday Evening Post* and *National Geographic*. The clean October sunshine came through the tall windows. I could hear the afternoon grow quiet as kids walked away from school; I could see them walking past the library, in pairs, in groups. Howie Sands shouted to Al Goodwin, telling Al he couldn't play football until later—he had to go to the A & P to buy some pumpkins for the seventh-grade Halloween party.

Even after I was pretty sure that everyone had left the schoolyard I sat at the table reading for fifteen more minutes. Then I left the library and started slowly up Garfield Street.

Old Miss Simons' house was silent. The birds were quiet—I supposed because the feeders were empty and there was nothing for them to chatter about. Outside the gate I paused, studying the front porch. I saw no movement there. The box of sunflower seed stood on the porch, beside the front door.

I glanced up and down the street to be sure no one was around. Quickly I pushed upon the gate, hurried up the porch steps, and reached for the box of seed. A dime lay on top of the box. I peered through the screen door into the hallway. The house was still, filled with shadows.

I carried the sunflower seed out to the side yard and heaped the bird feeders. I rinsed the birdbaths again and poured clean water into them. As I worked I kept glancing at the window overlooking the side yard, and although I could not see anyone standing there, I had the feeling that Old Miss Simons was watching me.

I put the box of sunflower seed where I had found it on the porch, and I placed the dime on top of it. Then, closing the gate behind me, I hurried away from Old Miss Simons' house.

On the following afternoon, when I returned, I found two dimes on top of the box of sunflower seed. For a moment I stared at the dimes as they gleamed in the sunshine; finally I picked them up and put them in my pocket.

Each afternoon for the next few days I went to Old Miss Simons' house and heaped the bird feeders with seed and filled the birdbaths with clean water. I discovered that the sparrows and blue jays were no longer afraid of me. While I worked, they fluttered around the feeders or swished about in the clean water in the birdbaths; then, on the fourth day, I saw the cardinal. Bright red against the yellow maples, the cardinal swooped about the lower branches, whistling full throatedly, then scolding in a short thin chip.

I turned toward the window, hoping that Old Miss Simons might be watching. Nothing stirred inside the house. The windows were closed. The cardinal perched on a branch in one of the maple trees, tilted his head, and observed me with sharp black eyes. When I stepped toward him, he darted from the tree, hesitated for a second on a birdbath, then fluttered into the air and vanished around the back of the house, trailing his short thin chipping sound.

The next day as I approached the house I saw Old Miss Simons sitting on her porch steps, in the sun. I paused with my hand on the gate, wondering if I was supposed to continue taking care of the bird feeders. Old Miss Simons beckoned to me. "Come in," she said. "The sun is wonderful this afternoon."

I pushed open the gate and found myself staring, in spite of myself, at Old Miss Simons as I walked up the porch steps. I could see that she looked pale, her skin almost transparent. Her long hands lay quiet in her lap, the fingers spread to catch the sunlight.

A new full box of sunflower seed stood on the porch. As usual, Old Miss Simons had put a dime on top of the box. I turned toward her, to tell her that I did not want the dime, but when I saw her sitting in the sun I decided to say nothing. I pocketed the dime and said to her instead, "We needed a new box of seed." Then I added, "I saw your cardinal in the yard yesterday."

Old Miss Simons looked up at me and smiled. "Isn't he beautiful?" She shook her head, "I feel guilty," she said. "I know the cardinal is my favorite simply because he's more handsome than the sparrows and blue jays."

"He sings nicer than the other birds," I said.

A blue jay fluttered past us, scolding raucously. Old Miss Simons said to me, "I've noticed that the birds are used to you, now."

"I'd better feed them," I said. Then I lied, "I'm in a hurry."

I walked around to the side yard and put handfuls of sunflower seed into the bird feeders, while the blue jays—a pair of them had appeared in the maple trees—scolded me. Sparrows fluttered onto the feeders, cheeping, scattering the seeds as they pushed greedily for sole possession of a feeder.

I emptied the birdbaths and frowned at the thick layer of algae that coated them.

I walked back to the porch. "The birdbaths need scrubbing," I said to Old Miss Simons. "If I had a brush . . ."

Old Miss Simons motioned toward the front door. "In the kitchen, on the shelf next to the sink . . ." And she added, "I knew they needed cleaning, but I didn't want to bother you."

I pushed open the screen door and stepped into the hallway, telling myself not to be curious about the inside of the house. I felt the silence close in on me. The house smelled musty. The warmth of the afternoon sunlight still clung to me, and I shivered as I felt the dampness in the shadows that filled the hall. I walked quickly to my left, into the kitchen. The kitchen sink was made of thick black slate. I had never before seen such a sink. On the wooden shelf beside the sink was the scrub brush. I picked up the brush and turned away, trying not to look around. But I noticed that there was only a single small pot on the stove; I saw the kitchen table, painted gray, with a single chair drawn up to it, the table set for one person. Everything in the house was arranged for a person all alone.

"I found the brush," I said to Old Miss Simons, as I walked down the porch steps into the sunshine.

I scrubbed each birdbath thoroughly under the spigot at the side of the house. I washed away the algae until each bath glowed white, then I placed the clean birdbath back on its pedestal, stepped away to be sure I had made it level, and finally I filled each bath to the brim with clean water.

"I've finished," I said to Old Miss Simons.

This time as I walked through the hallway into the kitchen, to return the scrub brush, I listened to the silence and realized how alone Old Miss Simons must be in her house.

I thought I heard her call to me. "What?" I said, starting out the screen door onto the porch. Had she caught me staring at her kitchen? Then I drew back, watching.

Old Miss Simons had not spoken to me. She was calling to the cardinal that was perched on the iron fence. The bird filled the air with its short thin chipping sound. Old Miss Simons extended her hand, in which she held a few sunflower seeds, and she called "tzip, tzip! tzip, tzip!" imitating the cardinal.

The cardinal fluttered from the fence into the rhododendron, swaying on the end of a branch, tilting his head; then he swooped onto the walk at the bottom of the porch steps.

"Tzip, tzip!" Old Miss Simons cried, throwing a couple of sunflower seeds to him.

The cardinal ate the seeds, scattering the shells, his bright eyes watching Old Miss Simons.

Suddenly I heard the sound of laughter, mocking. Howie Sands and Al Goodwin stood across the street, watching Old Miss Simons feed the cardinal. My heart sank.

If Old Miss Simons had heard them laughing she gave no indication. "Tzip, tzip!" she called to the cardinal. "Have another seed."

Guffawing, Howie and Al ran up the street, tossing a football in the air between them. I waited until the sound of their laughter had died out in the afternoon, then I pushed open the screen door and stepped onto the porch. The cardinal flew into the rhododendron, reappeared on top of the iron fence, and fluttered away.

Old Miss Simons turned to me, smiling. "Did you see him?"

I nodded, and at the same time I looked up the street to be sure Howie and Al were no longer in sight. I said to Old Miss Simons abruptly, "I guess I'd better go." I walked past her without looking at her. But after I had closed the gate and started away I glanced over my shoulder and could see her, slim, gray-haired, alone, sitting on the porch steps again. She seemed to be looking down at her hands, which she held in the warm October sunshine.

I saw Old Miss Simons again the next morning on my way to school. The weather had changed during the night, and now the morning was overcast and cold, with the first touch of real fall. A gray chill wind whistled through the trees and sent leaves tumbling over the ground. I had to hold firmly onto my cap to keep it from flying off.

Old Miss Simons, wearing a kerchief and a heavy sweater, was nailing part of a bird feeder to a tree. Scattered about the yard lay the shattered pieces of all the other feeders and the

broken birdbaths. Every feeder had been ripped from the trees and deliberately smashed; every birdbath had been overturned and shattered.

Trembling, I walked into the yard, stood silent for a moment beside Old Miss Simons, then said stupidly, "Who did it?"

She did not reply. I thought she had not heard me and I repeated, "Who did it?"

Old Miss Simons shook her head. She mumbled something about Halloween approaching. Clumsily she succeeded in fastening part of a feeder to the tree. Her hands seemed stiff with cold. Half a dozen sparrows, fighting the wind, flitted past us. Above us, in the maple, a blue jay complained. Old Miss Simons looked up, searching the tree. Almost mechanically, she rummaged in her sweater pocket and took out a handful of sunflower seed, which she placed on the feeder she had improvised.

I heard, behind me, the sound of snickering, and I wheeled around. Al Goodwin and Howie Sands stood on the sidewalk, peering over the iron fence and the rhododendron. Howie Sands shouted, "Tzip, tzip, tzip!" and he and Al slapped at each other, laughing.

Old Miss Simons turned to face them. As Al and Howie started to run, the wind whipped Howie's cap from his head. The cap came sailing over the fence and landed in the yard. Howie stopped short, perplexed, clutching at his bare head. He took one uncertain step toward the fence, then he stopped again. The wind rumpled his hair.

Al, still running, shouted to him to come on, but Howie did not move.

Old Miss Simons walked slowly across the yard, picked up Howie's cap, and without looking at Howie or speaking to him, she hung the cap on the fence. She turned away, rummaging in her sweater pocket again. She put another handful of sunflower seed in the feeder.

I saw Howie snatch his cap from the fence. He hesitated; then, scowling, he pulled the cap tightly over his head and walked away. After he had crossed the street he hesitated again, looked back, and at last hurried off.

In the distance I heard the five-minute warning bell ring out.

"You'll be late for school," Old Miss Simons said. "I don't want you to be late."

I nodded. "I'll be back to help you this afternoon, as soon as school is out."

A couple of sparrows flew down onto the feeder and pecked at the sunflower seeds.

"I'll go in now," Old Miss Simons said to me. "It's cold, isn't it? But the sun was lovely yesterday afternoon."

As I ran down Garfield Street, I remembered that I had saved all the dimes Old Miss Simons had given me. I had enough to buy a new bird feeder. . . .

Strether's station wagon hurtled through the countryside, past trees touched with October frost, past fields of shocked corn from which starlings and sparrows veered, startled by the sound of the passing car. We were on our way to Johnston's Woods.

Miss Folger-Robinson tugged my sleeve. "You've been so quiet," she said. She held out a handful of sunflower seed. "Try one. You'll like them."

I noticed that the Olney Bird Watchers, as they scanned the roadside for birds, cracked sunflower seeds between their teeth and chewed the kernels. I tried one of the seeds and found the kernel surprisingly sweet-tasting. "Why, it's really good!"

The Olney Bird Watchers turned and smiled at me. I looked at the seeds in my hand. "They remind me of a woman named Miss Simons," I said. "She was the first person I ever knew who was interested in birds. Everyone in the neighborhood thought she was crazy because she fed sparrows and blue jays. . . ."

VII

The Christmas Count

Up to the day before Christmas, it had not snowed. The low hills, visible from every window of the farmhouse, stretched lifeless and dreary against a horizon that held the threat of cold December rain. At the north boundary of the pasture stood a grove of Scotch pine, and the green of the pines was tinged with a gray color. Against the darkness of the pines, the naked sycamores leaned with lonely, skeletal whiteness.

My bedroom was cold and I knew I would have to heat water for a shave, so I pulled the blankets over my head and tried to forget the stubble on my chin and the uninviting morning outside my window. For a minute or two I was contented in my dark isolation; then I heard Sophie and Jake moving about in the kitchen, and I got out of bed, dressed, and hurried downstairs toward the friendliness of their voices and the warmth of the kitchen stove.

Sophie and Jake lived alone on the farm; they had offered me a quiet rest during Christmas vacation, a place where I could forget the long months during which I graded blue books, lectured in freshman English, and balanced teacups and sugar cookies at faculty gatherings. Besides, both Sophie and Jake were accomplished birders, and I had arranged for the Olney Bird Watchers to pick us up for the Christmas count: the farm lay on the edge of the fifteen-mile perimeter assigned by the Audubon Society to the Olney group. In that way I could take part in the count and at the same time spend the kind of Christmas in the country that I had seen only on Christmas cards, with the fireplace blazing inside, with the stars outside bright overhead, and the reflection of the lights from the farmhouse windows streaming out into the night across the snow. That kind of Christmas.

But, as it had turned out, Sophie and Jake would not use the fireplace because they had discovered four sparrows nesting in a chink in the chimney bricks. And the week had been marked with mild rain, more like spring. Jake generated his own electricity from a waterfall in the creek nearby, and something had gone wrong with the power. The water in the creek was too high to permit repairs, so at night we used two old kerosene lamps for light.

Then, last night, Sophie and Jake had received a telephone call from Bernie, their son-in-law; Sylvia was having a bad time delivering the baby. Sophie had decided to go to Columbus in the morning.

"A fine Christmas this is going to be," Sophie said, as I entered the kitchen. A cup slipped from her hand and broke in the sink.

In a wooden box next to the stove a mourning dove, startled at the sound, raised its small head and blinked its eyes at me. Two months ago Jake had found the dove with its wing broken; he had put a splint on the wing, swathed the bird in bandages, and kept it in the box beside the stove while the wing healed.

Sophie threw the pieces of the broken cup into a wastebasket and said to me, "We've decided that as soon as I'm sure Sylvia is better, I'll come right back and give Jake a chance to go to see her. That's the only way he'll be satisfied everything's all right. I'm sorry the Christmas we planned for you had to turn out this way, though."

The kitchen smelled of fresh coffee and Sophie's pancakes and maple syrup and homemade butter. Sophie leaned over the wooden box beside the stove and touched the mourning dove gently. She dried her hands, looked out of the window at the gray day, pulled the light chain beside the bulb over the sink, and then remembered aloud, "No electricity. I keep forgetting."

"I'll take care of breakfast and the dishes if you want to finish packing," Jake said to her.

I thought that worry and trouble had no business intruding

into a kitchen that smelled as good as Sophie's kitchen; it had no business touching people like Sophie and Jake.

Half an hour later Jake backed the pickup truck from the barn to the kitchen door. I carried Sophie's suitcase outside.

"I'll be back around noon," Jake said to me. "That'll give me plenty of time before the Olney people pick us up."

"Last year we counted forty-nine species in the area," Sophie said. She glanced upward at the sky. "I hope the rain holds off until the count is over."

I watched the pickup careen down the dirt road and out of sight. I was alone.

The morning air was damp. Underfoot the ground was wet with winter sogginess. Jake had turned the stock out, taking advantage of the mild weather to clean the barn. A dozen cows wandered complacently around the pasture. They stopped to stare at me while I stared back at them; but I felt uncomfortable and timid under their scrutiny. I picked up a stick and pretended to examine it. The cows turned away, browsing. The bell clanged from around the neck of the largest cow. The sound cut sharply through the gray morning air and drifted away into the pines that bordered the pasture. I looked out in the direction of the distant hills, as if I expected to hear the echo of the cowbell out there.

Mutt came lumbering up to me, and I realized it was the first time I'd seen the dog that morning. She was a large dog, part collie and part dog-in-general, and at the moment she was wide and low, carrying puppies that Jake had hoped to sell for Christmas. Mutt sniffed at my hand and at my shoes and then sat down, waiting for me to decide what to do.

We went for a walk. Out of sight of the farmhouse the road was more quiet than ever, with the only sound the damp rubbing of bare branches in the warm, December wind. For companionship's sake I said to Mutt, "It certainly doesn't seem like Christmas at all, does it? I wonder how the Olney Bird Watchers are doing on the count."

But Mutt loped her independent way several yards ahead of me, while as a protest I began to hum the carol, "Hark! the Herald Angels Sing."

At noon Jake had not yet returned to the farm, so I ate an early lunch alone, leaning against the edge of the stove. I made a ham sandwich for Jake; he would have it to take along on the Christmas count, if he did not return in time to finish lunch at home before the Olney Bird Watchers arrived. I walked to the window and checked the empty road and the weather. The warmth had gone out of the wind. I looked up into the sky and decided that the threat of rain might have turned into a threat of snow. The tolling of the cowbell in the pasture had a sharper sound, with a kind of chill in it. It seemed to me that since it was turning cold perhaps the cows should go back into the barn, and I wished Jake would return.

I filled the mourning dove's drinking cup with water and emptied a handful of grain into the tin from which it fed. Then, because I had nothing else to do, I let the dove peck a few grains of corn from my hand.

At a quarter to one the pickup truck pulled into the yard. I was putting more wood in the stove as Jake and a gray-haired gaunt man walked into the kitchen. Jake was excited; he introduced the man to me, but I did not get the name exactly: it sounded like "Hutchims." It was evident that Mr. Hutchims had been drinking.

Jake drew me into the next room and explained hurriedly that he had met the man in the railroad station at Middletown, after Sophie had caught her train. He remembered Hutchims vaguely as one of the series of hired hands that he had used years ago.

"Now I can get to see Sylvia right away," Jake said. "I'll have to miss the Christmas count, but I can't help it. You can drive me to the highway right now to catch the one o'clock bus to Columbus. Hutchims will take care of the farm for a day or so.

"It'll only take me a minute to pack," he added, as he disappeared into his bedroom.

"Well," I said to Mr. Hutchims, in the kitchen, "it was lucky you met Jake at the railroad station."

"Wasn't it?" Hutchims smiled. He filled the kitchen with a whisky smell that I could taste. "I was just hanging round the station. I been working in Bennertown the past six months."

"Oh?" I said, immediately uncomfortable: Bennertown to me meant the state mental institution.

"Six months is a long time," Mr. Hutchims said. Then, as he

saw the distress in my face, he added, "I was in charge of a group of guys at the hospital there, working as a guard, y'know. But this morning I got tired of the job and walked out, without even saying a word. Y'get tired of that kind of work."

"I suppose so," I said. But Mr. Hutchims had not convinced me as to what side of the fence he had been on; I thought he had a wild look in his eyes. "It looks like we might have snow for Christmas," I finished.

"Could be," Mr. Hutchims said. He held his hands out over the stove and then stared at the mourning dove in the box. "Jake tells me you're going out to count birds this afternoon with some people." He shook his head to indicate incredulity.

"The Christmas count," I said, defensively.

Jake came into the kitchen. He ate the sandwich I had put out for him and at the same time gave Mr. Hutchims instructions about getting in the cows, milking them, and watching the cow that was due to have her calf.

A few minutes later I was driving Jake to the bus.

"All he has to do is take care of the stock," Jake said. "I've got to see Sylvia."

"Sure you do," I said. "Wish her a Merry Christmas for me."

"Tell the Olney people I'm sorry about the Christmas count. I hope you get some good birding in this afternoon."

Jake hailed the Columbus bus on the highway, and I drove back to the farmhouse alone.

Mr. Hutchims was walking out of the yard carrying his suitcase. "Hey!" I yelled. I pulled into the driveway, leaped out of the truck, and ran after the departing Hutchims.

"Too much work here," Mr. Hutchims explained with a shrug. "I got lots of friends in Eaton. Think I'll spend Christmas with them."

"But I don't know anything about taking care of the farm," I protested. "You didn't even get the cows in from the pasture, and there's an expectant cow in the barn and any minute it might—"

Mr. Hutchims rolled a wild eye and proceeded down the road.

At that moment Strether's station wagon swung into the driveway. The windows of the car were wide open. The Olney Bird Watchers, wool-capped and ear-muffed, leaned out. Miss Folger-Robinson and the Gnomes waved.

"Forty-two species so far," Dr. Hurlburt called to me.

"Forty-one," Mrs. Hurlburt corrected.

I ran toward the station wagon.

"Forty-one species," Hunt said, rather grimly. "It *could* have been forty-two. I thought I heard a golden-crowned kinglet, but there was so much chatter around . . ." He glared at the women.

"We have the *two* children out on the count," Mrs. Ingraham said, pointing to the carrying cases she and Mr. Ingraham had tied to their backs. "Kathy and Robin."

"Are you ready to go?" Strether asked.

"Wait until I tell you what's happened," I said, shakily.

I told them as briefly as possible.

"Tsk, tsk," Miss Folger-Robinson said sympathetically.

"How awful!" Mrs. Hurlburt said.

Strether shook his head. "The man sounds crazy to me. Jake should have known better."

"I can't leave the farm, with no one around," I said.

The Olney Bird Watchers climbed out of the station wagon. They paused for a moment to look up anxiously at the leaden sky; they buttoned their woolen jackets, then, like good bird watchers, kept their mittened hands ready on their binoculars.

Strether's voice was irritatingly calm. "We'll have to think of something," he said.

"The children are awake," Miss Folger-Robinson said to the Ingrahams. Kathy, smiling, peered out of the carrying case on Mrs. Ingraham's back. Miss Folger-Robinson adjusted the muffler that Kathy wore. Mrs. Hurlburt hovered over Robin, who grinned from the carrying case on Mr. Ingraham's back. I retied the loose strings on Robin's hat.

"His first Christmas count," Ingraham said, rather proudly.

The Gnomes clucked.

"Good heavens," I said. My voice cracked. "I'll have to miss the Christmas count! The cows—milking—and one's expecting a calf . . ."

"I can take care of them later," Strether decided. "We'll stop on our way back from Greenwater Pond. I can do the milking then."

"I can't leave, not with Hutchims wandering—"

"Four English sparrows!" the Gnomes cried out, interrupting me. They pointed toward the roof of the farmhouse.

"They're the ones that live *inside*, next to the chimney," I explained.

Mrs. Ingraham made a notation on the check list, while Mr. Ingraham peered over her shoulder.

"That makes three hundred and twenty-eight English sparrows," Ingraham said. Turning to me, he added, "They're an official part of the Christmas count, so you've become an official observer. You haven't missed contributing to the count, after all."

I sighed, "Contributing, indeed."

"There's no rule about how *long* an observer has to be on the count," Strether said. "Your name goes on the list."

"The briefest bird walk in history," I said. "Four English sparrows.

"Wait!" I added, remembering suddenly. "The mourning dove!"

I led the Olney Bird Watchers into the farmhouse. We gathered in a circle in the kitchen and stared at the bandage-bedecked mourning dove which squatted, half asleep, in the box beside the stove.

"One mourning dove," Mrs. Ingraham said. "That makes a total of one hundred and four."

I pretended to feel better about the Christmas count. "Did you know that Jake used a pocket comb as a splint for the wing?" I said as we stalked out of the kitchen.

Outside, a few flakes of snow swirled in the cold gray air. Hunt frowned. "We'd better get to Greenwater Pond as soon as we can."

Looking up at the sky, Dr. Hurlburt nodded. "We need nine more species to beat last year's count."

I watched Miss Folger-Robinson catch a snowflake on the tip of her tongue.

"Ready, everybody?" Ingraham echoed.

Strether leaned out the window of the station wagon to tell me that he would bring the group back to help me as soon as the Christmas count was over; I was not to worry, not even about the expectant cow. "In the meantime," he said, "you can get the cows in the barn. Open the barn door and call them. They usually know where they belong."

The station wagon swung out of the yard. The Olney Bird Watchers already leaned out the windows alertly, binoculars in hand.

"Good luck!" I called. My breath hung in the cold air.

The car was gone. Silence fell over the farmyard. I felt a snowflake on my cheek. "The Christmas count," I said forlornly. "Well . . ."

A cowbell rang out in the pasture.

I turned, shouting for Mutt, hoping she could round up the stock. She was nowhere in sight, and I cursed her lack of responsibility. During the past few days I had seen Mutt, at Jake's order, chase the cows into the barn.

I opened the barn door and hallooed into the pasture. The cows turned and watched me, and I watched them. Then they started to move toward the barn, their breath visible in the chill air.

That was my moment of triumph—my only moment of triumph. Once inside the barn, the cows refused to march into their stanchions in spite of my shouting.

"Here!" I cried, holding open one of the stanchions, pointing. "Come on, now!"

The enormously expectant cow, blinking her wide wet eyes, turned in her special stall and stared at me, annoyed perhaps at the noise I made. Finally, one cow stepped into the stanchion and I clicked shut the bar around her neck. The others refused to follow her example.

Never before had I realized that cows could be so *huge*.

"Mutt!" I shouted. Nothing happened.

Then to save face I began to whistle tunelessly as I sauntered toward the barn door; I stepped outside and shut the door quickly behind me. I had at least succeeded in getting the cows into the barn.

Perhaps I should have gone out on the Christmas count with the Olney Bird Watchers, leaving the ungrateful stock to fend for themselves.

Anyway, nothing prevented me from going on my own Christmas count, as long as I stayed near the farm. I picked up my binoculars in the kitchen and started out, walking toward the creek at the foot of the hill that sloped away from the house. The roar of high water echoed above the bare trees. I leaned against the iron railing of the bridge over the creek and waited for some birds to appear.

The snow fell in scattered solitary flakes; there was no other movement against the gray of the afternoon. I trained my binoculars on a snowflake and studied its slow descent. I watched the flake touch a rock on the edge of the creek and melt; then I focused my binoculars on another snowflake, then on still another, and since no birds had appeared, I began to count snowflakes.

Once, I heard the sudden rustle of dead leaves and, startled, I searched out the source of the sound: a squirrel scurried up the bank.

The snow fell faster, and I noticed that the flakes no longer melted as they touched the ground. The quiet of the afternoon was more marked than ever; even the sound of the high water in the creek seemed muffled by the heavy snowfall.

Slowly I walked back to the farmhouse. In the stillness of the kitchen, grateful for the company of the mourning dove, I warmed my hands over the stove and watched the ground turn white.

Had the snow cut short the Christmas count? The afternoon was already growing dark. The lamps in the kitchen needed kerosene. I went out to the garage to get some.

I found Mutt there, and in the excitement of discovery I

almost dropped the kerosene can I was holding. I ran to Mutt in the dimness of the garage and bent over her. She was having her puppies! By my breathless count she had six. I had never before seen such new puppies.

Determined not to be helpless, I found a large piece of clean cloth, tucked it under Mutt's head so that she would be comfortable, and stroked her. Feeling a strange pride, I checked again the number of puppies. Six! A new version of a Christmas count, I thought. I ran to the kitchen and brought Mutt a pan of milk. She seemed content with what I was doing for her.

But the cows were not content. I heard the clanging of a cowbell inside the barn. A cow mooed, and I remembered Jake telling me that only discontented cows mooed. I hurried through the snow to the barn, threw open the door, and peered inside. The cows were clustered around the closed grain boxes. The cow that I had enticed into a stanchion was lying down: she was dying, I thought at once, for I had never seen a cow lying down just like that.

I ran out of the barn, and, shielding my eyes against the falling snow, I stared up the road, as if staring would make Strether's station wagon materialize. The road remained empty. I brushed snow from my shoulders, forced myself to count to one hundred—expecting something magic to happen—and peered up the road again. Nothing.

Heavyhearted, I returned to the barn, which looked crowded, with cows wandering around at will. They watched me curiously, their eyes mocking me. The cow that had been lying down was standing up. I surveyed her thoughtfully. For the past two nights I had watched Jake while he did the milking.

Could I? I wondered.

I took a pail from the milk room. "Nice cow," I said, approaching her. I put my hand on her side and patted her.

The cow swung her head around to stare at me, and it seemed to me she assumed the look of a martyr. At any rate, my first attempt at milking began. I had listened to the singing of the streams of milk as Jake directed them into the pail when he did the milking. But I could produce no such singing sound. The milk fell weakly into the pail. My wrists began to ache. My arms got tired. The cow moved, impatient. The pail slipped between my knees, I smelled barny. My fingers became clumsy. And, after

fifteen minutes of concentration, all the milk I could get was hardly enough to cover the bottom of the pail.

The kerosene lamp filled the barn with shadows. For the first time since the milking, the pattern of shadows from the stall in the corner caught my eye. Something had happened there. I put down the pail and carried the lamp closer to the stall. My heart began to race at the beauty of the sight: the cow was licking her new brown-and-white calf as it lay curled at her feet. Birth always seems a miracle, and the ease and acceptance of it on the part of the dumb animals around me—the cows in the barn had paused to stare—added to the magnificent simplicity of the miracle.

But as I watched the cow and her new calf a warning came to mind, the way warnings will at such a moment: something about finishing the milking of a cow once it has been started, or sickness will result.

And then, as I was about to run out to the road again, Strether's station wagon pulled into the yard.

"We did it!" the Olney Bird Watchers called to me. Miss Folger-Robinson waved excitedly, as if she were seeing me for the first time in years. "Fifty-one species!" she cried.

"Fifty-one!" the Gnomes echoed.

Dr. Hurlburt was the first out of the car. "The trip to Greenwater did it!" He pumped my hand in his excitement.

Mr. and Mrs. Ingraham stepped out of the station wagon, balancing their sleeping children on their backs. Mrs. Ingraham waved the check list so that it caught the last of the dusk visible through the heavy snowfall.

"The cows . . . !" I shouted to Strether.

With irritating composure Strether stepped from the station wagon. "Fifty-one species," he said cheerfully. He patted my shoulder. Then, kicking the snow from his shoes, he strode toward the barn. I trotted at his heels, and the Olney Bird Watchers trailed after me.

"Two more species than last year," Hunt said.

Inside the barn, Strether lifted a pitchfork from a hook on the wall and shouted at the cows. Instantly they started to amble toward their stanchions. The walls of the barn danced with the movement of their shadows. Strether glanced briefly into the stall of the newborn calf and then he disregarded it entirely.

"Oh!" Mrs. Hurlburt said, approaching the stall on tiptoe.

"Sweet!" Miss Folger-Robinson said, looking over the railing.

The Gnomes touched each other on the arm, and then, standing on their toes, they peered over the railing, too.

Mrs. Ingraham put her hand in Mr. Ingraham's hand.

Strether started milking. The streams of milk sang as they hit the pail, a wonderful sound to me. The cow in the stall had finished licking her calf clean. We watched the calf struggle to its feet and nuzzle against its mother, seeking food.

"It's a heifer," Dr. Hurlburt said.

"Perhaps we should reconsider the golden-crowned kinglet," Hunt said. "Now that I think about it, I'm almost sure . . ."

No one paid any attention to him.

"Kathy's awake," Mr. Ingraham said to his wife. "Let her see the new calf. Shall I wake Robin?"

Strether gave me a full pail of milk to empty into a can in the milk room. He worked quickly, sure of himself. The Olney Bird Watchers gathered around him, admiringly. The milk foamed into the pail that he held steady between his knees.

Half an hour later, after Strether had finished all the milking, I washed the filter and the pails in the milk room. Miss Folger-Robinson rinsed and hung up the pails. Strether and Hunt and I spread hay in the feed troughs for the cows.

"That's it for the night," Strether said.

The Olney Bird Watchers filed out of the barn. I closed the door.

"Now I can tell you about what we saw that was really special," Strether said, stomping through the snow toward his station wagon. He brushed snowflakes off his jacket. "A myrtle warbler!" he said, exultantly. "Just as we were leaving Greenwater Pond. I saw the yellow rump and—" He raised his hand in triumph.

"A *warbler?* In *December?*" I said.

Miss Folger-Robinson laughed. "You should see your face," she said.

"Fifty-one species isn't bad, is it?" Dr. Hurlburt asked.

Strether climbed into his station wagon, and the others followed him. They leaned out the windows. One of the Gnomes tapped me on the arm and whispered, "A myrtle warbler."

"I'll be back in the morning," Strether said to me. He started the motor. "Don't worry about anything."

Then, as the station wagon started out of the yard, the Olney Bird Watchers called to me, "Merry Christmas! Merry Christmas!"

And I remembered that it was Christmas Eve.

The station wagon disappeared down the road, the red taillight gleaming in the snow.

In the kitchen I looked at my watch and saw that it was suppertime. I was hungry and tired. I smelled of the barn, for all time. I fried a couple of eggs, and looked with a great deal of respect at the glass of milk which I poured for myself.

Sophie phoned from Columbus as I finished eating. Sylvia was better. She had had a daughter. Jake was standing at the phone and wanted to know if everything was all right back home. They were returning to the farm in the morning—Sophie wanted to make me a good Christmas dinner. How was I spending Christmas Eve in the country? And had I any reports of the Christmas count?

"A warbler," I heard her say to Jake. "They saw a myrtle warbler."

I told them that the cow had a heifer and Mutt had six pups, and a moment later we exchanged Christmas greetings and said good-by. I put down the phone. The kitchen was quiet, except for the sound the mourning dove made as it shifted its position in the box beside the stove.

I put a few kernels of corn in my hand and leaned over the box. The dove's bill tapped against my palm. When the corn was gone I ran my finger over the top of the dove's head.

"Christmas count—four English sparrows and a mourning dove with a broken wing," I said.

The snow had stopped. I put on my jacket and stepped outside, into the night. At the north end of the pasture the pines stood dark against the snow. The yard was white. I thought of the inside of the barn, with the cows secure and the new calf close to its mother; and I thought of Mutt and her six puppies; and I no longer felt lonely.

From the barn came the muffled sound of the cowbell; then the sound stopped and the world around the farmhouse was quiet again. Over the barn, where the clouds had broken up, the stars appeared.